The Summons:

A Salt and Light Anthology

Fairy tales by various authors

Edited by Evelyn M. Lewis

Table of Contents:

Foreword

The founding mission of Keepers of the Gate is to lower entry barriers for Christian authors to the world of publishing, in order to bring Christian influence and creative freedom to a now secular-dominated publishing sphere. Our goal is to preserve the values of literary excellence while bringing what has been called "Salt and Light" to the literary world.

Keepers of the Gate did not coin the term Salt and Light (a biblical reference) nor its conjunction with Christian literature. Instead, the term refers to a spontaneous movement of Christian authors in the literary sphere and their desire to build a cohesive body of work.

We at Keepers of the Gate felt this objective aligned with our goals as a publisher, and wished to signify our association with it, as well as represent the fact that the authors that are featured in this anthology arise out of this movement.

The Christian authors you will read today have brought to the table seven unique and original fairy tales.

Following in the tradition of greater authors like CS Lewis, whose fauns bowed down to Aslan, we seek to both baptize the fantastical, as the fairy Sindri is blessed by the holy man in *Addy*, and elevate the mundane to recognize its place in God's grand epic, as do the members of the Bible study in Maria Fedina's story *The Strange People*.

We hope that you too can experience the Christian life as a call to adventure. From all of us to you; please enjoy *The Summons*.

Addy

By R.C.L. Kamp

Once upon a time, there was a village on the outskirts of a forest that fed into a mighty mountain range. In this village, near the grassy meadow leading to the forest, was a cottage which housed a father, a mother, and a young girl named Adelina. Adelina, or Addy, as she preferred to be called, had her mother's eyes, her father's hair, and six years under her belt, and was known throughout the village for being a sweet, if shy, child.

Each night, as she was tucked into bed, her mother would tell her stories of far-off places and the wondrous residents of these lands, especially of the fairies. The fairies were said to tend to the flowers and herbs and small animals, as ordained since the world began, and rarely showed themselves to humans. They existed as a remnant of a different time, before the world was fallen, and so did not often interfere with the business of man.

Addy always asked if the stories were true, but her mother would simply smile and plant a kiss on her forehead, wishing her a good night's sleep.

The Summons

A Salt and
Light Anthology

Addy's life at that age was simple. She would help her mother with chores and play either in the meadow or with other children in the village. This simple life had a small but meaningful disturbance when, at one evening meal, her parents began mapping out preparations for a visitor – a special one, according to their anxious tones.

Their cottage was much like the surrounding ones – brick walls, a thatched roof, and a central fireplace in the kitchen. An adult's eye might notice a slightly higher quality of materials, as well as a spare room that the other cottages did not have. Addy only knew that the spare room was used for special guests to the village and that her family would always play host as a result.

Her parents' tone confused Addy, however, as they seemed to be particularly anxious about hosting this guest.

"What sort of guest is coming?" she asked.

Her father replied, "A wandering holy man will be staying with us, as of this upcoming week. A wandering holy man is like a priest or a prophet," he added, taking note of his daughter's very confused expression. "He goes around preaching and helping those in need – he's even able to perform miracles. He is on his way from the northern country to our capital, which will take him through the village. It is a great honor for him to come this way, as well as to host him."

"He also speaks to the fairies," her mother added with a teasing smile.

Addy pondered all of this information and grew curious as to the nature of their visitor.

On the first day of the new week, Addy and her parents made their way to their appointed meeting place, the well in the center of the village. There stood an older man whom Addy did not recognize, but whose presence felt familiar all the same. He greeted her parents fondly, addressing them by name, before turning to Addy.

"Hello, Adelina. My, how you've grown. I met you before as an infant, but of course you don't remember that." He smiled down at her as he spoke.

Addy grabbed her mother's skirt with one hand, but managed to stutter, "Hello, sir."

He looked delighted at her polite greeting and indicated to her parents to head back to the cottage.

As they did so, Addy studied the man seriously. He appeared at first like any ordinary common man – whether fisherman, carpenter, hermit, or teacher – but for his eyes. His eyes shone with an entrancing kindness and love towards all of creation. Yet his gaze also held something else – it seemed to pierce to the very soul with a confident knowledge of one's deeds.

As they made their way to the cottage, Addy watched how the others reacted to his presence. Most bowed their heads to him– in

9

The Summons

A Salt and
Light Anthology

fear or in respect. The children ran up to him with warm welcomes, while some adults shied away from his face entirely. They were stopped often by petitioners – people who desired to speak to the holy man for one reason or another, seeking wisdom, healing, compassion. The unrepentant petitioners – who would try to justify unjust deeds to themselves and to him – seemed to feel judged, with nerves raised the longer they stood in his presence. The repentant, however, found mercy and a refreshing of their spirits. He carried very little – a cloak, a small bag, and a small money pouch – but he had no fear of the future.

In studying him so intently, she nearly missed that they were now at the front door of their own cottage. The holy man blessed their home in gratitude for housing him, and then they stepped inside. Her parents fussed about making sure their guest was comfortable, while Addy took up residence on one of the chairs and watched. Eventually, the fussing was appeased, and the holy man joined Addy on another one of the chairs.

"You have been observing me very intently, Adelina. Is there something you wish to know?" he asked.

"Can you really speak to fairies?"

He laughed heartily. "Oh ho, if I can speak to fairies, then the fairies in your mother's stories must be true, yes? And if those good stories are true, then perhaps other good stories are true as well…" he trailed off, pondering for a moment, before smiling at her again. "Yes, Adelina, the fairies and I speak from time to time. Though they are still quite shy of most humans, so I would not go disturbing them unnecessarily. Do you understand?"

The following week brought on and off rainstorms, typical of the early spring. On a day the rain was more of a drizzle than a downpour, Addy set about one of her favorite activities – rescuing the worms from the well-trodden path. She moved from the muddy road to the fields of grass and wildflowers over and over, carrying a worm or two in her hands each time she did so. But on this occasion, when Addy gently released the worm into the grass, she saw movement from the corner of her eye. She looked— and there, under a white wake robin— was a figure, asleep.

The figure looked almost human— aside from his small stature and his wings. His skin was tanned from time spent in the sun, though his face lacked a certain rosiness of life. His wings were nearly completely translucent but for a slight tinge of blue. His wet brown hair stuck to his forehead and his clothes clung to him, damp. He looked feverish, even as he slept.

Addy approached him cautiously. She gingerly touched him with the tip of her finger to see if he would awake. He stirred, but remained in his feverish sleep. She poked him again, and though his face contorted in discomfort, he still did not awake.

Addy thought hard about how she could help him, trying to remember the last time she was sick. As she ran through the list– soup, tea, extra blankets – she suddenly recalled her father asking if she was warm enough. Gently, she moved the fairy, cradling him in her hands, and she quickly and carefully made her way back to the cottage.

She burst inside the cottage in search of a parent – instead finding both, as well as the holy man. Addy sputtered in surprise as she spoke, "L-look, a fairy. H-he was in the cold. It looks like he has a fever."

The adults all appeared taken aback for a moment, before the holy man gestured towards her hands. "May I see?"

Addy approached him and slowly revealed the fairy, who still appeared feverish, though the warmth of the cottage and Addy's hands seemed to be doing some good for him. He was beginning to stir, a slow awakening like that from a deep slumber. The holy man peered at the fairy before reaching into his bag and pulling out a thimble and a vial. He poured a drop or so of the vial's contents – a perfectly clear liquid – and proffered it to the fairy, who drank it and was quickly recovered. Within a minute of drinking his medicine, he was flying circles around the room. Addy and her parents watched, amazed at the miracle before them.

He paused before the holy man, hovering, and the movement of his hands indicated that he was explaining something to the man. When the fairy was finished, the holy man turned back to Addy.

"Adelina, Sindri thanks you for saving him. He says that he owes you a debt."

"Why? I was just trying to help him – I wasn't trying to put him in any debt."

"Yes, but you were kind to someone in need. You could have

presumed that another, whether human or fairy, would be along to help him. But you did not. You chose to help him – and he will not soon forget that kindness."

Addy still did not understand what he meant, but she did understand the fairy Sindri gliding over to her and hugging her shoulder the best he could.

[But] Jesus said, "Let the little children come to me and do not hinder them, for to such belongs the kingdom of heaven." Matthew 19:14

Addy

13

The Summons

A Salt and
Light Anthology

14

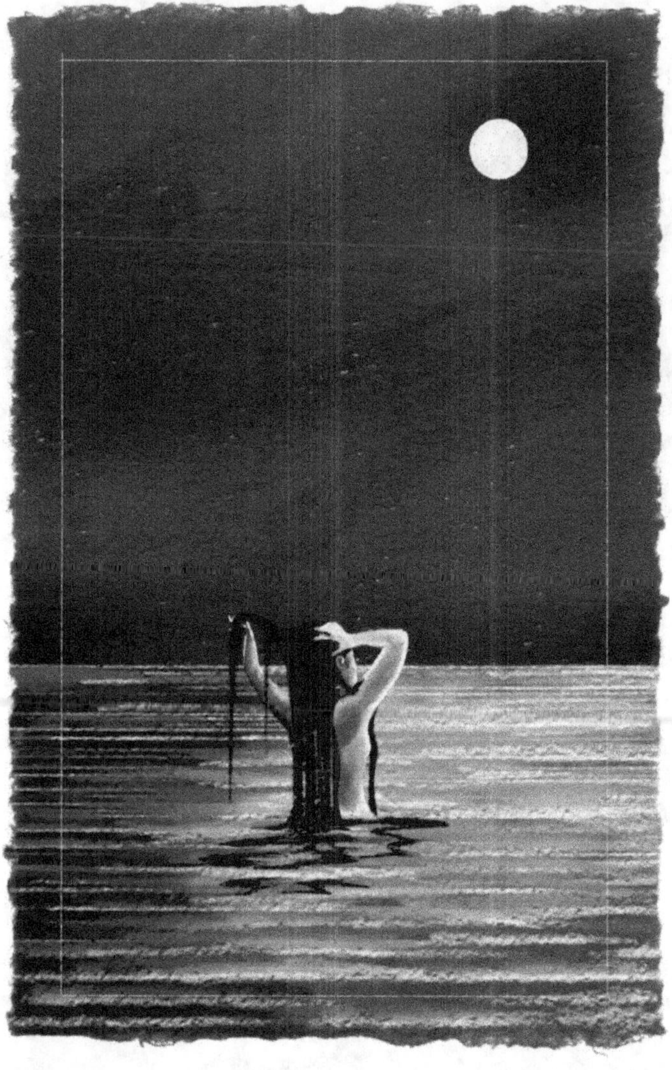

The Girl Who Chased the Sun

By Sydney Han

I n a cave beneath the sea, there lived a girl with scales. They were white scales, as pure and shiny as pearls, and they covered every inch of her body except for her head, from which floated her lank, seaweed-colored hair.

She lived alone in her cave. The fish that she ate had no voices to speak with her, and the only sound was the rumble of the undersea currents that moved her to and fro. Occasionally, a soft glow of golden light filtered down through the deep blue, glittering on mineral deposits in the stones that lined the ocean floor. The girl delighted in these lights, since they mirrored the way her own scales reflected light. She longed to see the greater light above that created them, but the water around her was so heavy and cold that it was hard to swim upwards.

One day, when the minerals were flashing and golden, she made up her mind to reach the light, and thrust herself off the grainy sand of the ocean floor. The water pulled at her limbs and hair, weighing her down, but she fought against it, and after a long time breached the surface. She bobbed for a few moments, looking all around her with great wonder.

The sky was as dark as the ocean, and there was no sign of the golden light. Instead, a pale silver disc hung far above her, as pure and pearlescent as her scales. Indeed, her scales reflected the light, flashing a thousand brilliant sparkles across the water. And the silver disc spoke to her!

"Child," it said in a low voice, "why have you come?"

"I seek the light," she said. Her voice was rough and gravelly, and the words hurt her throat. "Where is the light that is so bright it pierces the water?"

"Not now, not now," the silver disc sighed. "I am only a mere reflection. But in a few hours it will come, and you may see it then."

Satisfied, the girl sank back down to her cave. She slept all night and dreamed of golden warmth, and when she awoke, the minerals glittered!

Delighted, she raced up through the water, pulling against the waves, and burst out into glorious golden day! The sky was blue, brilliant blue, and no silver disc hung over her, but rather a giant yellow sphere so dazzling that she could not bear to look at it too long. She reached up to it in delight, hoping that it would make her scales as bright as itself.

Instead, the heat of it seared through her scales and into the soft white flesh beneath. Terrified and in agony, she began to cry.

From the sphere came a voice, melodic and haunting:

"Child, what do you seek?"

"You," she sobbed, but her voice cracked, and the word came out garbled.

She wept for her dumbness, but the sun reached down its hands to hold her. The intensity of its fire pierced her with delight, yet also agony. Despairing, she pulled away and dropped down into the waves.

Yet again tragedy struck! For the salt in the water stung her severely wherever the scales had been scorched by the sun, and her lovely white scales were black and burnt wherever the sunlight had reached. The skin beneath them flared red and hot, tender to the touch. Even her tears were salty enough to burn her cheeks, and yet she could not keep from crying at the pain.

Consumed by the sun, yet rejected by the sea! In anguish, she began to skim along the surface of the water, unwilling to sink down into the waves, yet unable to exist above them.

The sphere did not reach for her again, and for hours she labored forward. Then the water became shallower and pulled at her less, and sand brushed her feet once more.

She stumbled ashore onto a small, wooded beach. The light was fading behind her, the rays no longer scorching, and she crawled on hands and knees into the trees. It was dark here, dark and cool like her cave that she would never see again.

She sat on a patch of mossy turf and let her damp hair curtain her. The silver disc rose silently into the sky, but it did not speak to her again. For hours she watched from beneath her hair as the disc traveled across the sky. The light on the waves was as pale and shimmery as her scales had once been.

She dared to look at her burnt hands and arms. They seemed less harsh in the gloom of the trees than they had before, but tears still rose to her eyes at the sight of them.

Eventually, propelled by hunger, she began to hunt about her for something to eat. She moved deeper into the trees, away from the beach and the waves, and the sound of the surf washing against the shore faded into the soft chirruping of unseen creatures that hid in the darkness around her. The sounds were strange to her — high pitched, clear and sweet, unlike the currents she knew so well — but soothing. They did not remind her of all she had left behind. Still, they were not fish either, and oh how she longed for fish!

The trees thinned before her and she saw vast fields of gently waving stalks washed in the silver light. She dared to step forward into it with one hesitant foot. The light did not burn!

Emboldened, she stepped fully into it and lifted her aching arms. To her delight, there came no pain. With her hunger temporarily forgotten, she sprang forward and began to run. It felt awkward moving in air — too quick and too fluid, unlike the heavy pull of the water. Her hair felt strangely light where it dangled against her body. She ran down into the fields, exhilarated by her newfound freedom, and did not notice at first the stones underfoot that pierced her soft soles.

When she had exhausted herself, she slowed to a walk and began to grimace at the feel of sharp rocks rubbing against her feet. The silver light was fading away behind her, and a pale pink glow glimmered on the horizon.

Just as she realized what was happening— that the golden sphere was returning to torment her once more— she stumbled into a small village. There were only a few people awake and moving about. They gawked at her appearance, at the black burns and red flesh that striped her face and arms and at the dull tresses that hung down her back and over her face, then ran to cover her in their cloaks.

Exhausted, she let them lead her into one of their cottages: a cool, stone-carved structure very much like her cave. Their voices swam over her as she sank into a dreamless sleep.

She did not wake until evening, when the light was fading once more, and a dampness lingered on the ground. The farmers who had taken her in fed her salty dried fish — a new and not entirely unpleasant experience — and then asked her: from where had she come?

"From the sea," she said. "I chased the golden light, but it burned me." And she showed them her blackened arms and flaking scales, the skin raw and red beneath. They had never seen someone so injured by the sun, as they called the sphere, and they covered her in cool, damp clothes and let her rest again.

In the days that followed, as the farmers slept and the frogs sang in the streams, she sat often in the silver light of the moon. She watched it sink into her burnt scales, almost as if she were sucking the radiance into her. It did not hurt, nor did it soothe. Her scales remained as they had been since the moment they had encountered the sunlight.

For that, she hated the sun: hated its beauty and its terror, its glory and its mercilessness.

The farmers, whose skin had long since been browned by it, praised it for bringing life to their crops, and their wives praised it for sprouting the delicate green plants in their gardens, but she feared it for the pain it inflicted upon her. She spoke often, in her halting words, of the love she had once borne it for glittering on the rocks beneath the sea, and the villagers sympathized.

"Sit in the moonlight," some said. "The silver moon reflects the golden sun. Perhaps you may grow accustomed to the sunlight if you embrace the moonlight."

For some nights she did as they suggested, yet found no change in her reaction to the sun. It was as if the sun itself, offended by her fear, now spurned any association with her. A single hand held out to the palest of sunbeams would result in a fiery sensation rushing down her arm and into her soul. She cloaked her body in ever-thickening robes and wore a hood at all times to protect her face. She let her hair grow thick and wild around her face to further protect her from the dreaded brightness.

The days lengthened and the sunlit hours grew more perilous. She loathed daylight and wandered less, keeping to the safety of the stone houses. The villagers whispered behind her back and held council at noon when she was fast asleep.

"The sunlight here is too harsh," they decided. "She needs a place where the sunlight is gentle and filtered."

The emperor's men came in spring to collect tribute, and when they left, they took the girl with them. The villagers warned them to hide her from the sun, so she traveled in a coach draped in leather during the day. At night she stalked the edges of the camp, repelled by their campfires that reminded her too strongly of the sun.

The further inland they went, however, the brighter the sunlight became. When they reached the hill-country in which the capital city stood, she had doubled her layer of cloaks and refused to step foot outside the coach until dusk had fallen.

The capital city! What a glorious place it was! Seven-tiered it stood, and built of shining white stone. It was a brilliant beacon set among the rolling green slopes of the hill-country, and the peak was crowned in golden domes that covered the emperor's residence.

The emperor was away on business that summer, but his son graciously welcomed their strange visitor into the palace. He offered her free range of the gardens, which were covered in tinted glass to keep out the stronger rays on especially sunny days, and for several weeks she wandered the sprawling rows, lost in a sea of flowers and fruit trees and great, leafy bushes that were so large she could take shelter in them. They reminded her of the ocean, as the wild forest had done, and for a time she was content to live beneath the glass roof.

It was here that the moon spoke to her again. She was standing near one of the windows in the early hours of the morning, placidly watching as the golden dawn crept toward the city, when the moon whispered from behind:

"Child. What do you seek?"

"I seek nothing," she said, and meant it. The prince provided her with shelter and food in exchange for her company when he grew bored or weary of his court duties, and the garden provided her safety and comfort.

"But you are still looking," the moon murmured. "You cannot give up your love for the sun."

"I do not love the sun, nor does it love me. It burned me so!" And she flashed her arms. The pure white scales which had reflected the moonlight so brilliantly were dull and grayish-black now. In some places, the scales had fallen off to expose the rough, reddish-brown skin beneath. "It has made me hideous."

"You look like the others now," and the moon faded away as the sun rose.

Angered, she stood defiantly as the sun's rays filtered through the glass. She held out her hands to it and watched the light dance across her fingers. No beautiful scales reflected it, but her skin seemed to soak it in and warm from it. The realization came to her that she, too, could bear the sun— but only if her scales were gone and her skin darkened.

"It burns," she told the prince later. "And I do not enjoy burning. I want to remain as I am— or go back to what I was! I was happy then."

The prince gazed at her with soulful eyes. "You may find happiness still," he said simply. "But there is no going back. We can only go forward."

As autumn drew near, heavy cloud cover rolled over the city and dropped torrents of rain. The sun was hidden for days, and the girl left the safety of the garden to wander the streets. She still wrapped herself in her robes to hide her hideous form, but she enjoyed being among the people. Their voices were full of joy for the rain, and hope in the return of the sun afterward.

"How can anyone love the sun?" she asked the prince that night. "It hurts so terribly."

"It burns, yes, but it can heal too." The prince unfolded a book of medicine and showed her. "Some diseases become less harmful when exposed to sunlight. Some are even destroyed altogether."

"Then why did it burn me?" she asked in despair. "I am not a disease!"

The prince thought about this for a long time, his chin perched on his brown hands. "The sun burned away your scales," he said at last. "And then your skin became like ours."

"But it hurts—"

"Change always hurts." The prince looked at the maps scattered around the study, the books he had opened and marked up, and the letters from the emperor that lay on his desk. "But we must embrace it if we wish to move forward."

She did not like his words, and avoided him for a week afterward. In that week she often dreamed of her cave under the sea: the peaceful days of listening to nothing but the rumbling currents, of watching pale golden light flicker off the minerals at her feet, of raw fish and heavy limbs and empty, open space all around her. No voices, no sunlight, no pain. Every dream brought her awake with tears and an aching, hollow loneliness that she could not dispel. The garden held no beauty for her any longer, and ever against her will, she found her eyes turned to the horizon at dawn.

At last she returned to the prince's study and told him that she wished to go further east, toward the sun where the rain did not fall.

"If it hurts, so be it," she said, and clenched her brown hands beneath her robes.

"I shall come with you," he declared. "If you must suffer, it shall not be alone."

So they took leave of the palace under cover of night and rode over hill and dale, valley and vale, until they reached the mountains in the east. Only pale watery sunlight filtered through the heavy clouds.

"If we go up the mountain, we can get above the clouds," the prince said.

They left the horses to return to their stables in the city, and began the long climb up the steep mountain trails.

The paths were slippery and treacherous; often the prince took her hand to keep her steady on the rocks and mud. As they climbed, the air grew thinner and thinner. Her lungs, even though they had become accustomed to the air in the city that was lighter than the water she knew so well, gasped and ached for every breath. Sweat rolled like rain down their faces.

At last they emerged from the clouds onto a plateau near the top of the mountain. A full day had passed since they had left the city, and night fell around them in deep shadows. They made camp and slept deeply, exhausted from their journey.

The girl awoke first. She sat in the morning dew in her dark robes and watched as the flowers lifted up their faces to the first gentle touch of dawn. The sun began to rise, a golden-pink line against the pale blue sky, and she rose with it.

Hands clenched, limbs trembling, she walked to meet the sun.

For the second time she heard that haunting, melodic voice:

"Child, what do you seek?"

"You," she whispered. "No matter where I go and how I hide, I cannot turn away from you."

"Even if it hurts?"

She set her jaw and lifted her arms. The robes slid from her body and she stood in the sunlight, white scales scattered among the ashen ones, reflecting and absorbing light in equal measure.

"Yes."

The sun threw down its hands and she ran forward with her hands outstretched.

The sunlight blazed against her remaining scales until they turned black and wafted away as dust in the wind. The skin beneath reddened immediately, and then turned brown, as brown as the skin over her hands and face. She cried out in anguish, tears streaming down her face, and leapt up, up, up toward the sun.

In a moment all her scales had burned away, leaving only the clear brown skin behind, and her hair streamed out behind her in a torrent of fiery crimson. The sun caught her in its hands, wrapping its brilliant blazing rays around her, and her feet never again touched the earth.

The prince awoke to her cries and saw her disappear into the white-hot face of the sun. He stood aghast for a long moment, then stumbled forward to the pile of robes she had left behind. As he shook them out, a single white pearl tumbled out and rolled across the grass. It was the last of her tears.

He took it with him, carried against his heart, when he returned to the city. And he told the guards, and the council, and everyone who would hear, that the girl who chased the sun had found it at last.

The Masque of the Ald-King

By Elianna Swan

*I*n the days of long ago, when the moon was still a young hero walking the earth, the Ald-King ran rampant among the people of the world. None could turn but would find him wreaking his harm behind their backs; none could speak but would worry that the one to whom they told their secrets was truly him in disguise. Under his reign the world was rife with mistrust and sorrow.

Then a young hero arose, and her eye was clear and sought truth. She met the Ald-King in a great duel, clashing with him for three days and three nights without rest, until the hero summoned her last strength and cast the Ald-King into the shadows of the forest, and bound him there.

But she had been deceived, and the Ald-King at the same moment flung her into the sky with her own strength, and with the power of her selfsame binding bound her to the firmament.

So they hold one another in place still: the hero's ever-watchful eye shining silver in the night, pinning the Ald-King to the shadows where he lurks— and holds the hero in the sky. And though the hero's eye closes once a month to take the rest her mortal body yet needs, the Ald-King never dares stray far from the forest to which she has him bound.

As centuries have swung past, and men have lived and wed and died and forgot, settlements have crept closer and closer to the Alder Forest. None remember why it is called so, and they have named its pale and slender trees for the forest's name. The nearest village has been named Moon's Watch, and none remember the why of this either. But the moon remembers, and keeps her watch. And the Ald-King remembers, and weaves his schemes. And time swings on.

Lina walked among the fabrics in the shadowy warehouse, letting her hands glide over the silks as smooth as water, the linens soft as wind, the cottons light as clouds.

"Would that I were among the grand ladies who will wear these as the richest gowns," she sighed aloud. She caressed a blue damask that shimmered in the half light and imagined herself in a gown that flowed like a river and splashed around her feet as she danced in a glorious hall.

"Get thee to thy chores, girl," came her mother's voice from the door. Lina snatched her hands to her chest and whirled around.

"But, mumma—"

"Ach, just go on, dear. I will not tell ye again how much work I have yet to do to set these fabrics on their way. Get thee gone. And don't stomp!"

Huffing, Lina skittered from the warehouse and stomped through the yard to the house, splattering her hem with mud.

Could her mother not leave her alone to dream for one moment? Must she always be pursued by endless, thankless tasks, tasks which would never in a thousand years allow her to wear anything more glamorous than wool?

The wind sighed through the trees, drawing Lina's attention to the forest at the edge of the field behind the house. There the green branches draped like skirts, their leaves like patterns of damask, and the darkness beyond the trees was thick as velvet. She felt herself drawn, and before she quite knew what she was doing she found that her feet had taken her to the very edge of the dark woods.

Here something whispered to Lina, though she could not have repeated its words. She only understood a sense of sumptuous beauty, waiting somewhere beyond the trees for her to don it. She let her feet take her one more step, crossing from the field to the forest.

At once, a shadow peeled from a knot of slender white trees and wound itself into the shape of a man. He wore a fine set of courtly clothes and a crown of gems as red and shining as blood. Lina gasped and turned to run, but his voice when he spoke was so gentle that her fear blew away like a wisp of smoke.

"Lina. Wait."

She turned back, trembling. "Who are you, strange sir?" "I am the king of these woods, and I have asked you here that I may give you an invitation." He made her an intricate bow. When he straightened, an envelope sealed with a seal red as rubies appeared in the air before her, as though the wind held it out to her.

With a hesitant hand she took it, broke the seal, and slipped the parchment from its sheath. For a brief moment she could not read the glimmering letters, and then their meaning surfaced:

THE ALD-KING
LORD OF THE FOREST AND SHADOWS
REQUESTS THE HONOR WHICH THE PRESENCE OF THE LADY
LINA, THE BEAUTIFUL
WOULD BESTOW UPON HIS HUMBLE COURT
THIS NIGHT OF NEW MOON, AT
A ROYAL MASQUE

Deep red roses twined over and around the words, rendered in such intricate detail that Lina could nearly feel them prick her fingertips. She held the invitation in both hands, enchanted by the way the roses breathed and the lettering glimmered.

"The festivities will endure for three nights, until the moon unsheathes its sickle blade once more," said the Ald-King. "I hope that you would honor me by staying at my palace for that time."

"Why me?" asked Lina, when she had found her voice. "I am only a weaver's daughter. I am no princess, born to walk a king's halls."

"You are a beautiful thing, harboring a love for other beautiful things. I wish to bring you near to them."

She made to return the invitation to him. "I— I have nothing to wear."

He stepped closer to her, clasping her hands closed over the invitation. "Worry not, dear lady. My palace is filled with wardrobes that burst with fine gowns as bright as your eyes. They will be yours to dazzle my court with. Only come."

Oh, she wanted to. How she wanted to. She let him hold her hands, feeling the delicate strength of his fingers, the coolness of his skin. His eyes were earnest and glimmered gold like the letters on the parchment; his smile was hopeful; his doublet the most elaborate brocade she had ever seen even among her mother's best. One could get lost in a labyrinth like that brocade.

"I will come," she said with surety. There could be no question.

He squeezed her hands and his smile widened before he loosed his grip and let her go. "Follow the letters when they shine for you," he said. "They will show you the way to me. And be careful in the forest, for not all my subjects are kind."

And before Lina's very eyes, his shape wavered, a gust of wind stirred the draping leaves around him, and he became unformed, once more indistinguishable from the shadows of the trees.

She held the invitation tightly, feeling the imprint of his hands on her hands fade. A king, clearly the sort of king from a fairy story, wanted her to attend his masque— not only that, but he had offered her beautiful clothes to wear. It was an answer to her dearest wish, and she only longed for the new moon to come quickly. Night's velvet would smother the crescent in but two days.

Two days. She could be patient that long.

When night fell on the second day, she was ready. She had laid the invitation open on her bed and dressed herself in her Sunday best, which was only a linen thing, but she could not bring herself to wear her woolen daily to the palace gates of the Ald-King. Now she sat on her bed and watched the gold lettering glimmer in the candlelight, waiting. She held her breath as her mother's footsteps progressed down the hall and the door of her room shut. Minutes passed. An hour. Perhaps only seconds.

Then she awoke, in the dark hours before dawn.

Horror shot through her and she bolted upright in bed. She had missed it. He had not come. He had never been real at all. Tears swelled in her heart and streamed down her face, before she saw something that made her gasp and cease her weeping.

The invitation lay on the bed before her, still glowing, though the candles in her room had long since burned out. Then one glowing letter fluttered free of the page before her. Another followed, then another, until the golden text of the invitation floated in her dark room like so many fireflies.

They drifted to her window, trailing light. Wrapping herself in a cloak, wiping her face, Lina followed, slipping through her curtains after them into the cool summer night.

Without the soft light shed by the letters she would have been hopeless to see her path. The moon's eye was shut, and the few stars that flickered above her were pale. At the forest's edge the lights continued blithely into the trees, but Lina hesitated. The yawning depths were like the mouth of a sleeping animal, half-open and harmless— but if it woke?

The lights drifted on. If she did not follow now she would lose them, and lose her chance. So she shook off such thoughts, and into the forest's green dark she plunged.

It was a thin and weed-tangled path that the lights led her along. Greenery caught at her ankles and stones wedged under her feet, but Lina, uncaring, fought to close the distance between herself and the leading lights. She had almost reached them when a voice spoke close to her hear and startled her to halt.

It was not the voice of the Ald-King. "Lina, return home."

She picked up the path again. In the dark her feet were uncertain. The lights drifted on ahead, dancing in a curve.

"Return home, Lina. The moon cannot keep you safe tonight. Return home."

A tree branch tugged at her hair. To the right she heard the soft chuckle of a stream. The ground tipped down like the deck of a ship as the lights led her into a valley.

"Lina…"

The voice was softer now, weaker. "...return home…"

The Ald-King's lights drifted down into the center of the valley, then all at once swirled up into the air as sparks when a new log is thrown on the fire. Brighter and brighter they flared until, by their glow, Lina saw a magnificent palace take shape out of the night.

Its walls glimmered black as the depths of a hidden pool. The golden lights had set themselves like gems all round the great door, which was carved to depict scenes of dancers and joyous revelry. Looking at it, Lina almost heard its music, and her feet forgot their tiring journey and longed to dance. She reached for the door to knock, but it swung open before she touched it.

A hall full of light bloomed before her, and the light came not from any lamp or torch she could see, but suffused the very air. Across the room two staircases soared up from either side and met one another high above. Instead of the chandelier she had always imagined would decorate the halls where her mother's fabrics went to dwell, the Ald-King had a ball of glittering snowflakes swirling at the apex of the vaulted ceiling. Below her feet ran a carpet of thick moss dotted with tiny purple flowers, and the air hung with the scents of sweet fennel, fairy-skirt, and winter cherry.

"Lina."

A shadow landed lightly on the mossy carpet at the top of the stairs and there the Ald-King stood, a cloak billowing up behind him like wisps of green smoke. He descended the stairs with his arms thrown wide in welcome. Lina held herself straight and smiled in return, hardly believing she was truly here.

"In coming here, you honor me," he said as he reached her, grasping her hands warmly in both of his. "You are perfectly on time, for my other guests will not arrive ere the coming day has faded again, which will give you ample time to peruse the finery and find that which suits you. The day, my lady, is yours."

"My lord," she said, curtsying, "it is I who am honored by your attentions. I know not what I have done to earn the gift of your favor, but I do treasure it."

He beamed. "Come with me."

The Ald-King led her along a maze of halls somehow richer than the entrance hall below, hung with paintings of landscapes rife with magic and tapestries that shimmered with life.

The chamber he showed her to was one of the turret rooms overlooking the forest side; the village of Moon's Watch was not visible from here. The glass windows sheened with threads of gold and reflected the lavishly carved wardrobes that lined the room, each, she imagined, brimming with the most magical dresses she would ever see. Directly opposite the door, a vanity sparkled with jewels and chains. Lina's feet sank into the plush carpet as she gazed and gazed.

"Here I leave you, and anything you find is at your pleasure. I eagerly await your appearance when the masque begins." And he bowed, and left her.

The moment the door closed Lina sprang for the nearest wardrobe and flung it open, drinking in the riot of colors and textures and styles within. She ran her hands over every gown, her heart throbbing with glee, and moved to the next wardrobe, then the next, then the next, until every one in the room was wide open and singing with color.

Once she dared try one dress on, she could not stop. She saw herself in taffeta, in silk, in damask and satin and organza, crimson, turquoise, emerald, lapis, a dizzying whirlwind that left her breathless and laughing. All she had ever wanted and more was here, piled at her feet, and la! She had not even gone to the masque yet. She regretted that she would have to go home when the nights were over.

As she thought this, she heard a faint tapping somewhere in the room and paused to listen. There, again— tap, tap, tap. Moving through the room, she tried to place the source of the sound, but the rustle of the gown she wore made this impossible. She stood still in the center of the room, turning her head, discarded gowns strewn like a riot of flower petals around her.

Tap, tap, tap. It was too deep a pitch to be the window, too muffled to be the door. Then she had it. It came from one of the wardrobes— the only one she had not emptied, because its gowns were dull colors like grey or brown or white. She went to it and pushed the gowns aside, and the tapping sounded again, right against the back of the wardrobe.

"Hello?"

Tap, tap.

Lina tapped in reply and found that the back of the wardrobe swung away from her touch, revealing a dimly lit staircase leading down. But no tapper stood on the stairs, and when the sound came again it came from far down, out of sight.

"Hello?" she called again, but only the tapping answered.

The candlelight in the stairway had a friendly, confiding quality to it, and Lina was not afraid. She had plenty of time before the masque; she would miss nothing, and perhaps this was some clever surprise orchestrated for her by the Ald-King. So she lifted the skirts of her gown and descended the staircase in pursuit of the tapper-elusive.

Eventually, the steps gave way to a wood-panelled passageway, which in turn became a tunnel of beaten earth slowly encroached upon by moss and grasses and flowers. She seemed to walk for hours, and would have turned back were it not for the constant reassuring glow of the candles. Because of them, when the path became more and more overgrown she simply raised the skirts of her gown above the dirt and followed after the tapping.

The sounds of morning began to mix with its rhythm, and Lina heard the musical cry of lake-loons and the chittering of squirrels and, briefly and far away, the low of a bull deer. A chill breeze stirred the trees and coaxed dayblooms to open to the sun's first searching rays. And the tunnel of earth ended in a curtain of willow fronds.

Lina pushed them aside as she had done the dresses and emerged into the clearing, into the grey and gold of early morning. The tapping sounded again from her left— she turned to see a little grey bird beating a nut against the branch it perched upon.

"Oh, you odd thing," she said, half-laughing. It looked up at the sound of her voice, tilted its head, and abandoning the nut, flew down to land before her, bobbing its head as if bowing.

Still laughing, Lina swept into a curtsy. "You are a strange creature. Did you call me here to wish me luck? Or to congratulate me on my wonderful good fortune?"

The bird fixed her with its beady eyes, spread its wings, and suddenly a woman stood in its place, a woman whose dress with its voluminous sleeves was as grey as still water at dawn. Her hair was grey also, falling in soft waves to her waist, and her face was aged and kind.

"Daughter," she said, "you are in danger here. I see you wear the garb given you by the Ald-King, but it is not yet too late. Come with me, Lina. I will bring you safely home." And she outstretched her arms.

Lina drew back, clutching her skirts. "Who are you?"

"I am the Queen-That-Rides-The-Winds, the ruler of the air and all who fly upon its strength. I and my brethren serve the moon and take up her watch whenever she must set it down." Still she reached out, beckoning Lina closer. "I mean you no harm, child, but the Ald-King does. He is no true ruler here. He is a prisoner, and ever he seeks to escape, or if he cannot escape, to make his imprisonment more bearable. Either spells ill for you."

"No," said Lina, shaking her head. "No, he is kind. He sees me. He has given me a wonderful gift."

The Queen's gray eyes filled with sadness. "He lies, Lina. But I see you will not come with me now, and I will not force you, but I beseech you to accept a gift from me, as well as a word of advice." And taking a silver blade from within her robe, she cut off one of her own long draping sleeves. She set the piece of fabric on the wind, and the wind brought the flowing thing to Lina, who caught it and held it up.

In the wind it had become a dress of no fabric she recognized— simple, grey, and feather-soft, little more than a shift with sleeves to the elbow.

"Wear it instead of the gowns the Ald-King provides, that he may not cast his thrall over you."

Reluctantly Lina draped the dress over one arm. She had no intention of wearing the thing to the masque; it was worse than the dress she had slept in yesternight. But perhaps this queen-woman would leave her to return to the Ald-King's palace if she thought Lina would listen to her.

"And, last, the advice: ask the Ald-King for a basin of pure water to be sent you, that you may wash and prepare for each masque. Yet instead dip the rich clothes he has offered you into the water, and through its lens, see whether they be truly fine."

Giving no answer, Lina backed away through the willow hangings. When she turned away from the woman, she found herself not inside the tunnel or the stairway up, but just inside the wardrobe, standing among the white and brown and grey dresses she had passed over. She fingered them now. Though their colors had not attracted her, their make was elegant, and the fabrics were seeded all over with pearls or silver beads or amber. The dress given her by the woman— the Queen-That-Rides-The-Winds, as she had called herself— was softer than these others, true, but boasted not the slightest decoration. She hung it in the wardrobe, where it floated with arresting grace, as though threads of wind lived in its weave. Yet she turned away.

She went to the window and gazed out through the hazy gold of its glass. The sun had risen over the forest and burned away the mists of morning; she must have been gone from here for hours. No matter, she had hours still, and she spent them in sorting the gowns she had left strewn over the floor, hanging them in place again, choosing her favorites. The one she had worn through the passageway went in that wardrobe beside the wind-dress, and she shut the door firmly and chose another gown to wear. As she sorted and smoothed and spun in gown after gown, she marveled that she felt no hunger or thirst, even as the day slipped through the long-shadowed afternoon and into evening. Finally it came time for her to actually dress for the first night of the Ald-King's masque.

The gown she chose was red as the gems in his crown, red as the seal on the letter he had given her. The sleeves were sheer and clung to her skin like rose petals, and the skirt rippled like a cascade of fire and wine. For shoes she found a pair of slippers the jewel-bright red of pomegranate seeds that fit her as if made for her. Then she took herself to the vanity where she stained her lips and chose golden chain bracelets, necklaces, earrings dripping with rubies like a fall of blood. As she turned to see herself in one of the many mirrors— a vision of red she was, of fire and passion and love and wine— she realised she had no mask to wear.

A knock sounded at the door.

"Coming!" Lina's voice was unfamiliar to herself, lower, almost husky. She opened the door.

The Ald-King flung his arms wide. "I behold a most ravishing vision. At last is your beauty honored with its right and proper raiment." He took a small bundle wrapped in cloth from his doublet and presented it to her in both hands, and she accepted it, folding back the cloth to reveal an elaborate golden masquerade mask.

"Far be it from me to want to hide the barest scrap of your allure, but it is a masque, after all."

"Thank you. It is beautiful." She laid it upon her face and felt it mold to the curve of her cheeks, the arc of her nose. It fit itself perfectly to her with no part out of place, yet something in its movements as it adjusted to her made her uneasy. She brushed the feeling away and smiled at the Ald-King.

"Lovely," he said, offering his arm.

She took it, and he swept her away to another world. The ballroom was a swirl of faceless fey dancers, of music that entered her blood and became part of her and drew out part of her into itself. She was passed from partner to partner, and, laughing, she let the weaver's daughter slip away, left behind bit by bit in every step of the dance, replaced by this golden-faced princess of roses and vibrant fire. For hours, days, uncountable years she exhilarated in the feeling of newness, of intoxication. This night would never end, and with it she would dance on and on forever.

Then the music seemed to hush, until she could no longer tell whether she heard it or only felt it in her veins. Her feet slowed and stopped. The ballroom and all the dancers in it spun round and round her in a wild carousel, and she looked out across the room and met the eyes of the Ald-King fixed on her, and in them there was a strange light. The spinning of the dancers seemed to wind around her, tighter and tighter, as though she were a spool and they the thread. The ecstasy of earlier faded from her.

Then she looked down and realized her own feet were still dancing, carrying her deep into the spiral, and the music rose high and filled her head like wine. When she looked again at the Ald-King he was smiling, and the light was only candlelight.

Later, when the guests had vanished one by one and the first grey hints of dawn were soaking through the sky, the Ald-King offered to accompany her back to her chamber.

At the last moment after he bade her goodnight ("or, rather, good day"), just before he closed her door, she asked him if a basin of pure water might be brought to her.

His body stilled. She watched him, afraid, exhausted, wishing she had not spoken. But he only said, "Of course, my lady, it will be so," without turning to look at her, and closed her door behind him.

When the water appeared she did not notice. She had gone to the wardrobe where the wind-dress hung and was pondering it before she turned, intending to cast off her red gown, and found the silver basin sitting there.

The water was glazed with steam. Without a thought she stripped the dress and jewelry, struggling for a moment with the bracelets, and slipped into the water. It was warm and the curved basin held her like an embrace. To her surprise, she began to cry, and then her head dropped back and she fell asleep.

She woke shivering, though the water was still warm. Standing, she took up a towel from the floor which must have appeared with the basin, dried herself, and drew on a loose blue satin gown. Her own feelings were a mystery to her, and her neck ached. She went again to the wardrobe and stared at the wind-dress, touched the sleeves, ran her hands down its skirts. Then she pushed past it to touch the back of the wardrobe and watched the panel swing open.

This time the walk did not feel as endless as it had the first time. She brushed aside the hanging willow leaves and stepped once more into the clearing, looking around for the Queen-That-Rides-The-Winds. Instead, she saw a man as spindly as deer's limbs, wearing soft brown hunter's clothes and a haunted expression in his wide, liquid eyes.

"Child," he said hoarsely, "the danger is even greater." "Who are you?"

"I am the King-Betwixt-The-Trees."

"Where is the Queen-That-Rides-The-Winds?"

"Elsewhere. It is my turn to make a gift to you, though my advice will be the same as hers." He knelt down and began to unlace his boots.

Lina watched with distaste as he slipped them off and tossed them to land at her feet. He jumped at the soft sound they made thumping down in front of her, then gestured for her to take them up. Reluctantly, she did. They smelled of earth and sweat, but they were soft, almost velvety.

The King-Betwixt-The-Trees stood on bare feet, poised on his delicate limbs as if ready to flee, and said, "Wear them in the stead of the shoes the Ald-King provides, that he may not cast his thrall over you."

"Cannot I come with you now?" Part of her was not yet certain she wanted to, but she found it odd that he had not asked when it had been the Queen's first words to her.

"That opportunity has passed, Lina. The time to run will come. Return here on the morrow and the third ruler will be here to offer his gift."

"Who is the third ruler?"

But the King-Betwixt-The-Trees did not answer. His delicate limbs trembled so violently she thought they might shatter.

"Night falls," he said, his breath quickening. "I must go." And he leapt through the trees and vanished among them.

Indeed the light was fast draining out of the day. She held the boots slightly away from her body and went back through the passageway to her chamber.

The red gown lay discarded on the floor beside the basin. Setting the boots on the wardrobe floor beneath the wind-dress, she went to it and gathered it up, studying the ruffled organza. Then she held it over the basin and slowly lowered it in, watching the skirts balloon on the water before drinking it in and sinking below.

For a moment nothing happened, and then the fabric started to change.

First it grew heavy, heavier than the wet gown itself should have been, and she let go her hands and let it fall. The ruffles unwound and flattened and to her shock, uneven patches of mangy hair began to sprout all over the dress, until the once-elegant gown became a pile of strange animal skins.

She reached out a tentative hand and grasped the patchy sleeve, recoiling from the feel of the rough wet fur. And she dragged the whole mess out onto the floor. Horror crawled over her body, over every inch where the dress had touched her all last night. It was a horrible, wretched thing. It looked like a mass of dead creatures, sewn all haphazard together. Were they all like this?

At that thought she tore off the blue satin she wore and dropped it in. No, they were not all the same— the blue satin became a thing of empty scales, of shed snakeskins. When she drew it out of the water and dumped it on the floor it crumpled and fell to pieces.

She began to cry again, flinging dress after dress into the water, turning them all into their true and repulsive forms. Soon she was surrounded by cast-off snakeskins, husks of crickets and spiders, mounds and mounds of dead and balding animal skins. With tears streaming down her cheeks, and sobs hitching in her throat, she turned back to the wardrobe.

The wind-dress floated, drifting, gently alive. The boots below it rayed warmth and welcome. Lina went to them and dressed herself in them, and looked at herself in the mirror, shoulders slumped in defeat. The cut of the dress was plain. The boots were dirt-dusted. She herself was tearstained and swollen-faced. And the second night of the masque was upon her.

Again she went to the vanity and stained her lips and chose jewelry. The sleeves of the wind-dress ended at her elbow, so she stacked bracelets up the length of her forearms. She wound herself about with waist-chains and draped her neck with pendant and pearl. Finally she laid the golden mask upon her face and studied the result in the mirror with relief.

The sparkling necklaces and bracelets distracted from the drabness of the fabric and the waist-chains accentuated her where the dress's cut failed so to do. The rinceaux of the mask spiraled inward and made her eyes into pools of enchantment. The boots she could do nothing about. She spun in place for herself, almost recapturing the giddy anticipation of yestereve.

The Ald-King's knock came at the door and she went to it, cracking it carefully to slip out without letting him see within. His eyes flicked up and down her, and his gaze hardened, but he said nothing and offered his arm to her.

All night she fought sickness. The ballroom and the dancers' insane whirligig made her stomach turn and twist, and the intoxicating music made her head throb. But she was not pulled along in the current, for the boots she wore anchored her feet and kept them her own, and the dress uplifted her and made her too light to be dragged away. The draw of the dance met her and went through her, without displacing her. But all night she felt the Ald-King's unsmiling eyes burning on her until the first guests began to dissipate. At the first chance she slipped among those leaving and made her way to her chamber.

The sight of scattered decay met her at the door, and revulsion and despair rose in her throat. Part of her— a foolish part— had hoped that it had been a trick of some kind.

She picked her way across the room to the vanity, peeled the mask from her face, and made to shuck off the bracelets encircling her arms.

They did not move. She grasped them, wriggled and tugged, but with every effort they only tightened until she screamed in pain and panic, clawing at them. She wrenched at the necklaces until they choked her, strained against the waist-chains until she thought they would cut into her skin. Sobbing, she stumbled back and fell into the basin of water, writhing, restrained, sure she would drown.

But the water calmly worked itself between the metal and her skin, and she felt the chains loosen and slip off. She opened her eyes under the water and saw the jewelry morph into rats' tails and spiderwebs and then dissolve.

Shakily she stood, and stepped dripping out of the basin. Her arms burned with scratches, and the boots she wore were so heavy with water that she bent to take them off.

This time when she stood, she saw a glimpse of herself in the mirror, and her breath caught. The wind-dress was no longer flatly grey; instead, the shimmering water had imbued it with the opalescence of mist. She turned and turned before the mirror, openmouthed at the quiet splendor she had been given to wear. The dress caught the soft light falling through the window and held it like a gift, hummed with it like a song. It was beautiful.

Now her mind was set. She laced the boots back onto her feet, heedless of the water's weight, and approached the wardrobe. But when she pushed against the back panel, nothing happened.

No. She pushed again. Again and again and again. Panic crawled up her spine again and seized her mind in both its hands, and she flew at the wardrobe, beating at it with arms raw from where she had tried to claw the bracelets from her flesh. She had been foolish; she had been warned; she had been given every chance, and was it too late? Was something terrible going to happen to her, only for wanting something beautiful?

Sobs tore at her throat and she rushed back to the water basin, cupped her hands, and flung the water at the wardrobe, to see it burn through the false clothes like acid. She pressed her wet hands flat against the back panel, tears streaming down her face.

And it swung open.

Breathless with relief, she flew down the passageway and burst through the willow fronds into the clearing. The figure there turned, and she beheld an odd creature, not unlike a human, but decorated with strange gills and crinkles. Its body was ivory white, it was crowned with a wide-brimmed rounded cap, and it was wrapped in a cloak made of white webbed material. She stared until it spoke quietly, in a voice that seemed to come from many different directions at once, a many-layered whisper.

"I am King-Under-The-Roots, he that brings forth life from death, though I would that you live a fuller life before I must so transform your shell."

She crossed her arms tightly before her chest, feeling unease. "King, can you help me return home?"

"I can." It raised one arm beneath its cloak, bringing the strange fabric close to its face, and blew, sending white spores floating through the air toward her. They settled on her neck and chest and shoulders, clinging there, growing together to form a pelerine of living, lacelike webbing. She touched it wonderingly. It felt spongy, but not unpleasant, and it was light against her skin.

"A gift, and now, advice. Tonight, you must forgo a mask, hiding not your face when you go to the festivities."

"But… it is a masque," she said.

"Have done with foolishness," it said harshly. "Do you not feel your name fading? The thrall is on you yet."

She fell silent.

"Tonight, the last night of the masque, the Ald-King will begin his festivities early, as soon as all light has faded from the day. For at midnight the moon's eye will sliver open once again, and she will resume her watch over him, and his power will wane. This is when you must run. The dress of the Queen-That-Rides-The-Winds will speed you on, and the boots of the King-Betwixt-The-Trees will keep your feet sure."

She touched the pelerine at her throat. "And what will this do?"

"No harmful hand can touch you while you wear it, but in the palace of the Ald-King its power will steadily drain away. You must not dally when the time comes to run."

"Run where?"

"Out of the palace, out of the valley. From there, we will guide you. As will the moon."

In her chamber for the last time, she stood before the mirror. She had brushed water from the basin over the wind-dress so that it shimmered, and over the pelerine, which had taken on a lustre like pearls. Her hair she had wound into intricate braids, crowning her head. She left her lips unstained and the mask abandoned on the vanity. She had not given it over to the water. She could not bear to see what repulsive thing had been clinging to her face.

Tonight she went down to the masque without waiting for the Ald-King's knock. Though the sun had only just disappeared behind the trees, the music and dancing had already climbed to a frantic pitch. She braced herself as she entered, but she need not have; spores rose from the pelerine and formed a shield around her which the music could not penetrate, nor the dancers draw her from. Through it she looked and saw the Ald-King at the doors, searching the crowd with burning eyes, and she hung back against the windows. Outside, night had fallen in earnest, but no sign nor sliver of the moon could yet be seen.

"There you are." The Ald-King appeared by her side, taking her arm and turning her toward him to appraise her. "My lady, I am hurt that you reject my gifts."

She swallowed. "I felt myself…become less of myself as I wore them, as I danced. Forgive me, but I think I do not belong here, lord."

He laughed. "Sweet child, is it only this? Dance with me." His hands closed on her waist like the chains she had worn yestereve and he drew her to the center of the floor. She lost the thread of time, frozen in his gaze like a leaf on a lake in winter.

"Of course Lina the weaver's daughter does not belong here," he said, spinning her, "but you? Princess of silks, of the golden face?"

From nowhere he produced the very mask she had left on the vanity and clasped her to him, holding it before her eyes. "You belong here, decorating my palace."

The mask twisted and writhed in his hand, stretching out golden tendrils toward her face.

She tried to wrench away, but his hold was sure. He smiled a wolfish smile.

Where is the moon?

Then the clock struck the midnight hour, and the pelerine pulsed with a wave of spores. The Ald-King released her as if stung and she broke away, and ran.

Out of the ballroom and through the entrance hall she fled. The spores repelled the dancers back to clear her path, until they were all left behind her and she was bursting through the grand doors into the valley. Stars teemed in the sky like fireflies, but of the moon there was yet no sign.

The wind found her now, flying at her back, pushing her along with breathless speed as she ran up the slope of the valley. The boots guided her feet to land between roots and leap over rocks, each step swift and sure through the overgrowth. She did not remember the way, and fear beat in her throat, but she trusted to the forest-rulers' gifts and did not slow.

As she crested the verge, she heard the music crash to a stop behind her. She flung a look over her shoulder and saw the other guests pouring out of the door, morphing into the dark shapes of animals, and heard a wolf's howl touch the night. She plunged into the trees ahead.

Here she felt the presence of the Queen-That-Rides-The-Winds and the King-Betwixt-The-Trees even more strongly. Wings brushed her cheeks and arms, and she felt the slender form of a deer bounding beside her. With their help, her feet found the clearest path and raced along it, spores trailing in her wake and choking the creatures that tried to pursue. And at long last the eye of the moon shuttered open, a shaft of pale light sliced the night with the sure grace of an arrow, and the path gleamed silver at her feet.

The trees opened. Lina stumbled out. And there, across the glimmering meadow, glowed the windows of her mother's house.

A gust of wind swirled once around her body and blew through the trees behind her. She sensed the dainty presence of the deer as he stopped and let her run past him into the grass. Turning back, she saw a cloud of spores hovering at the forest's edge, stirred by the wind, blurring the spindly deer-king from sight.

"Go," soughed a voice that came from everywhere.

So Lina followed the bar of moonlight through the meadow-grass, slipped inside her house, leaned her back against the door. Bolts of fabric lined the hallway, but she passed them all by and walked to her mother's room to knock on the door. It swung open at her first touch, almost like the wardrobe passageway.

Her mother gazed at her, saying nothing, then all at once pulled her into a hug. Lina melted into the embrace.

"I made something for thee." Her mother's voice was rough with held tears. She led Lina to her own room, where the window had been closed, the bed made, and a pale blue dress laid at the foot of it, shining like water.

City of the Sun

By Guinivere Locke

I t was a time of Science, of Universities and Education, of Knowledge and Industry and Censuses, of Elite Students With Money to Spare and Wisdom to Disperse, and of Academicians Analyzing War With Numbers and Forecasting Doom. The Gilded Age blazed forth cynical beings into the world, and soon, the shadow erupted.

The shadow came first from the north. A coal miner in Virginia emerged from his mine to see it crossing the sky, and mistook it for the smoke of the northern city factories, until it lingered in the air and turned all to a dull, smokey grey. None knew what it was; all spoke of it and whispered ideas and told stories of divine vengeance and retribution. Scientists theorized and calculated and gave half-baked counsel.

The girl who saved them all was not one of these scientists— she did not, in general, concern herself with the theories and counsel and whispering. She knew what the smokey grey was and what it threatened the further it spread and the darker it grew. "It's the Night," she told her parents as they came in from the tobacco fields, worn and weary and, like their daughter, more concerned with how much knitting she had gotten done and how much she could sell it for than the smoke in the air from the north. "It's the Night and it will swallow us all," she insisted, "and drown the stars."

Her father gave her a kind, warm smile. "That's wonderful knitting, Loretta," he said. "Old missus Sanders will pay good money for that, come winter." The girl stopped talking about the Night, but while she knit, her eyes were turned toward the stars and the slowly creeping Night. The Night seemed to turn even her knit socks and blankets and sweaters into something darker and duller. She found herself looking forward to knitting less and less with each day.

"A big storm coming," her mother sighed. In town, others echoed it wearily· "Those clouds don't bode well at all."

That night, in that moment of dark when all the stars should be burning their brightest, the first star disappeared.

Sleepless children and weary parents looked up to see not a bright, comforting glimmer, but an opaque, black darkness in its place. The night after, two disappeared, then three, and every day the sky and the air and the town and the mountains grew more grey, more dull, more dim.

It was time for someone to do something, and as the politicians promised relief for votes and huddled in their large houses, and the scientists forewarned death and destruction and published their memoirs, and historians tracked Progress to this point, Loretta knew that she was the one who must act.

So one morning at dawn—a dim, grey dawn like all the rest now, with not a hint of pink or gold on the horizon—she rose earlier than her parents, took a knife and a sack of food and set out for the Other World.

Everyone knew the Other World existed, but finding the entrance was a fickle process, full of hardships and danger and risk. Loretta might never find it. But the Other World was their only hope—nothing in this one could stop the Night from devouring the stars. All the stories ever told about the Other World spoke of it as a place of hope and light, and if nothing else, This World needed some of both.

Loretta diverged from the well-worn paths and made her way through the distant forest, where she searched for days. She followed the trickle of a river, and the deer's faint tracks, until she came upon a house in the center of the forest—an old house, but polished and looked after as though brand-new. The girl stepped in.

Before her lay empty rooms and a long hallway lined with many doors, each one plain and unassuming but for the wood they were made of: a bright rose-gold mahogany. Loretta hesitated; she knew that if she chose the wrong door, she may never return to her own World at all.

Tucked into a nook of the empty room to the right was a tall spiraling staircase, and thinking that she might find more information upstairs, she stepped onto it. Up the long spiraling stairs she went. Many stairs and many hours had passed by the time she realized soft yellow sunlight shone through the windows she routinely passed, though it had been dark in the forest. "Such a strange place I have found," she said to herself, and continued, her heart lightened by the sunlight, which she had seen so little in the last few days.

Eventually, the stairs led Loretta to a landing that opened onto more rooms, all of which were empty, save one which had all the furnishings of a well-loved bedroom, papered with blue sky and brilliant stars. A bed sat in the center of the room, and in the bed lay a pale, still man in the last years of life.

The man caught her gaze, his own piercing and sharp. "I," said he, in a croaking, gritty voice, "am the Keeper of this House. I have none here to keep me. Would you, girl, get me a drink of water from the kitchen?"

Being frightened, but at her heart a kind pitying creature, the girl left the room, trekked several hours down the stairs, filled a cup she found in the kitchen with water, and trekked back up and into the room. The man had fallen asleep, and she woke him. "That's better," he said. "It is quite lonely here all alone. Would you tell me a bit about yourself before you go?"

And so Loretta, quite wishing to leave and continue her quest, but seeing that it was truly lonely in this house, told him stories of her mother and father, and of her childhood on their Virginian farm. The man nodded and listened, his blue eyes as piercing as ever and seeming to take her measure. "Those are good stories," he said. "A simple life. That is what I would like for myself." He sat and placed his feet on the wooden floors and shivered. "Please, would you go to the living room and grab me my dressing-gown? I feel up to leaving this bed, only it's so cold."

The girl kept her sigh to herself, and trekked several hours down the staircase, grabbed the dressing-gown from where it lay cast across the back of a chair, and trekked back up to the room, her legs feeling much more tired than they had as she walked through the forest.

"Now," the man said as he pulled on his dressing-gown, "would you assist me down the stairs? And while we walk, you may tell me why you have come into the House of Worlds and what you hope to find somewhere else that there is not here."

Loretta linked her arm with his and took excruciatingly slow steps down the stairs. "The scientists and professors speak of the End and of lost hope and of retreating underground," she said, "but that is not what we need. This world needs light and wonder, and I want to push back the Night that is falling at least for some little time. There is but one star left in our sky, and I must not let it be overtaken."

The man looked curiously at her. "Then you want the Other World. That is a perilous land."

"But it may have what I need."

"It certainly will." He sighed. "But if you are to go there, you must remember what you hear as we descend these steps, for it is only with my song that you will remember your aim." And he proceeded to sing a soft, repetitive melody, singing of trees and farmland and cotton-mills and newspapers and orange groves and dark pine-coated mountaintops.

Loretta listened, and found at the end that she could remember the song, as long as it had seemed, as though it had been imprinted on her brain.

Sunlight still shone through the windows onto the stairs as they stepped off the staircase and into the long hallway. The man stretched and groaned, reached over to a row of long keys in the hall, and took up one. "I shall grant you what I can, which few are so lucky as to be offered—here is the key to the Other World. The door you want is the third on the right. Go destroy the Night."

And so the girl unlocked the door, and turned the knob, and found her way to the Other World with much less fuss and bother than many.

That World, as the stories tell, is beautiful, and its very beauty entraps visitors, enchants and binds them, and makes them forget the sights and sounds of their own World. However, the song the Keeper had sung to her was still fresh in her mind, and Loretta hummed it to herself as she went along. The door had brought her out upon clifftops rising over glittering, endless seas, and as she traipsed over them and descended upon shores of silver sand, Loretta sang, seeking always for a sign, something she could put in her pocket and use against the Night.

In That World, it never grew dark, but stars wheeled above her next to the sun, like little specks of sunlight that had broken off and made their own way through the sky. A scent filled the air, something like sea brine and the freshest breeze she had ever smelled in her World. As Loretta wandered, she found that she could slake her thirst by way of freshwater pools and her hunger by way of berry-bushes, and as the endless, beautiful day continued, the song the Keeper had sang faded from her mind.

In the far distance across the silver shore was a forest, and the girl headed toward it. She realized suddenly that she felt very alone, on this broad seashore with not a single person in sight.

The girl entered the forest. It was much like the one in which she had discovered the House of Worlds, but lighter and free of shadows. The undergrowth was green, and small birds greeted her with song, which lightened the shadow of loneliness that had fallen on her. She followed a path, and came not to a House of Worlds this time, but to a derelict castle, crumbling into ruins and long ago abandoned. In the sunlit courtyard, there was a stone bier, and upon it lay a girl. As she stepped closer, she noticed threads of fine gold thread wrapped around the girl's wrists and ankles and braided into her hair.

Loretta stopped uncertainly, but the girl's eyes opened. "Oh! Finally," chirped the girl joyously, "It's been so long since I've seen anyone here. Are you going to rescue me?"

"Rescue you?" Loretta hung back. "What do you mean by that? Who are you?"

"I was once the Queen of a distant kingdom, but my cousin, a witch, cursed me not to step outside the castle grounds until such a time as someone who has neither seen nor spoken the name of my kingdom rescues me—quite an impossible demand then. There was no market in a thousand miles which did not sell our cloth, and no glassmaker which did not claim that their glass did not shine like the light of our windows underneath our sun."

"*Your* sun?"

"Yes, or at least that was how we saw it. The sun hung directly over the kingdom, shining upon our windows and warming our cloth and feeding our great gardens and forests." Loretta, whose own sun certainly did not do such a thing, was at a loss for what to say, and before she could explain that she came from an entirely Different World, the Queen frowned. "Is it really so unknown now? Anyway, my cousin was a jealous girl, and thought she would make a much better Queen than I. I have had nought to do but sleep; after all, the birds do get tiresome after four centuries."

"Four centuries!" exclaimed Loretta. "That must be awful. I am quite busy, though. Do you know where you would go if I rescued you?"

The girl-Queen shrugged. "I suppose I would try to make my way back to…to my kingdom. I shall see if my cousin's family has really done better than I would have."

Loretta thought about simply asking her the way out of the forest and leaving her to her centuries of sleep. Surely Loretta could not be the *only* one for miles who had never heard of a kingdom so far away. But she was the one who was there, and the girl seemed so young, even if she was really four centuries old, and Loretta found she could not stand the idea of showing up and then leaving her again. She sighed. "All right. I'll see what I can do. Have you had anything to eat?"

As the girl shared some of the berries Loretta had collected as she walked, Loretta inspected the gold thread looped about her. It wasn't tied tightly, but it shone with something unique to this world.

Magic, thought Loretta. Out loud, she wondered, "How does one rescue a Queen from an enchantment, anyway?"

The girl raised a wrist. "This thread is the symbol of the enchantment. I can't cut it or break it—and I've certainly tried."

"Well," Loretta said, "sometimes breaking the symbol is the same as breaking the thing itself." She reached out and took hold of the thread and, with a firm yank, it snapped and fell to the ground. She did the same for the others, and then unbraided the Queen's hair.

The girl tip-toed tentatively to the threshold of the garden gate and reached out a leg to put it across onto the road. A flash of gold, and the girl was standing on the road, open-mouthed and gaping.

"It worked! It really worked!" She looked, in her excitement, more like a Queen than she had laying on the bier, red-cheeked and joyful and fair-haired and laughing and skipping in an ancient fine dress unworn by time. Her name, she said, was Berev, and then Loretta introduced herself, and they felt like they really were on the way to true friendship.

They walked to a fork in the path together, and taking the split heading east, the girl-Queen told Loretta more of her curse. "I used to rule over the kingdom of Kingsmere. Where I am now is unknown to me, for my cousin cast me into a far-distant country. No one has ever visited the castle before, in all the time I have languished there. If we can find our way to my kingdom, you will have all I can give you."

Thinking of her quest, Loretta found this very agreeable. Perhaps there would be something in that kingdom that she could use in her own world. As they walked, she told the Queen of her Own World and of the Night, and of her hope that she could hold it back in some way.

They followed the path for a long time, tracing through deep undergrowth and clearings filled with flower-clusters, between tall, thick oak trees. Eventually, Loretta realized that the birds had gone silent, and no animals rustled amid the grass or raced across branches. As the girls walked, a heavy taint of unease fell upon them, so that walking grew slow, and the air wavered with heat. Loretta sang her song again, remembering her time on the lonely sea-shore, and the Queen took the song up alongside her, and it rang out as the only sound in the forest.

Only a few paces more, and they found themselves before a

half-hidden cave tunneling deep into the earth. They entered, thinking that perhaps they might find refuge from the unease which had fallen upon the forest aboveground.

They soon realized that they would find no such thing, but by then it was too late. The cave led through a gently descending tunnel and into a wide cavern that stenched of decay, nearly hot enough to scald their lungs as they breathed.

Then the darkness was broken; the girls' eyes were met with all manner of bright, sparkling things—jewelry and crowns and gemstones. "This is a dragon-hoard," Berev whispered, and even as she said the words a large golden eye blinked up at them from the midst of the piles and her voice died in her throat.

The golden eye blinked up at them. The piles shifted and one long golden talon emerged, extending from a large foot that alone was twice the size of Loretta's head. From somewhere beneath a heap of coins and chalices, a voice, dark and resonant, sounded: "One of you is from here, and the other is not. What business do you, stranger, have in my cave?"

Loretta glanced at Berev beside her, but the girl, for all her bravery, seemed to recognize that the question was for Loretta to answer. Mustering all her own bravery, Loretta spoke up. "I am not from this land, O Mighty Dragon of Gold and Wealth. I do not mean to disturb your peace, only we felt anxious wandering so far through the forest, and hoped to find respite here." She said nothing of their unease above, for she had realized that it must have been a sign of the dragon's presence below.

"It is no disturbance. I appreciate a challenge, and Other-Worlders present the best." A long snout arose from the coins as the dragon twisted to peer more carefully at Loretta. "Where do you intend your path to take you, in the event that you do leave my lair?"

"Only through this forest and to the great kingdom of Kingsmere, O Dragon of Wonder and Majesty."

The golden eye flashed, it seemed, with a physical anger like fire. "You are in league with the King of that land, of course! My great enemy, who has sought to slay me and take my rightfully-claimed hoard for his own! For that aim has he sent you."

"If this Other-Worlder is in league with anyone, it is I, O Great Dragon," Berev said, stepping forward, "I who was once Queen of Kingsmere, but have not been in that land for many centuries. We have no quarrel with you."

The dragon hummed. "You, distant Queen, lie. I heard my enemy's song sung in the land above. I have little patience for liars, and dragons wake ravenous. Kingsmere is many leagues east of this land, down the Great West-East Road, distant and remote where the sun lives in all its brightness. There is no hope of getting there or of being found. For four hundred years, many have traveled down that road and I have swallowed them up. You, from such a distant land, would not go amiss any more than they." He reached out with one talon and scooped up the Queen, who went motionless with sheer terror.

"Wait!" Loretta strained her brain for something to say.

"Great Dragon, of the Magnificent Golden Scales and Talons Stronger Than the Mountains," she stammered, "we are no liars, but speak what we see as truth—though of course you in your wisdom may know better than we. The song was given to me by a man outside This World, whom I doubt knows anything about you, Wondrous Serpent. A distant Queen my friend may be, but she *is* my friend, and I believe I would miss her quite desperately if you were to eat her! I have heard many stories of the hospitality of dragons along with those of terror, and would you not rather have those stories spread about you so that you might receive ever more gifts and honor?"

The dragon regarded them suspiciously, but she had sufficiently flattered him. He looked at the Queen in his grasp for a long, considering moment, but placed her back onto the ground, where she stumbled and fell, looking more shaken than Loretta had yet seen her. He burrowed his snout—and those long, wicked teeth—back under piles of coins. "My hospitality is great, indeed, and I would not have it said otherwise. Remove yourselves from my sight, and do not return here again."

Loretta agreed (with a bit of reluctance and regret that she must leave so much gold and jewels to a dragon's keeping) and the dragon sank back into his hoard. A moment later, he had fallen asleep, and the cavern filled with the truly terrifying sounds of a dragon snoring. The girls stood there, terrified to move lest it be a trick, but after a long, still moment, they relaxed.

Though the entrance was not so far, the walk was tense, each girl expecting to feel those long golden talons in their backs. It

was only when they broke out into the bright sunlight that they relaxed.

"I do feel a little bad for him," Loretta said a bit sadly. "He was quite polite."

"Feel bad for a dragon? He would have been polite and courteous as he dropped us into his mouth and stripped the jewelry from my bones," dismissed Berev. "What was that he said about Kingsmere? It may be far away, but if all we must do is follow the Great West-East Road, then it could be a straight walk. There was no road when I was Queen, but it seems this road goes east for a ways."

Loretta agreed to follow it, and they went off through the forest, still a bit shaken by their encounter with the dragon.

On they went, and they passed out of the forest. Still, night did not come; the sun shone bright and gold, and the stars speckled the sky around it, and Loretta did not feel tired or weak as she might in her Own World, but went on with a light heart as she could never remember having had before.

They passed over wheat-fields and waded across babbling rivers and saw the sun get somehow larger and larger. At long last, Loretta and the Queen reached the gates of a large city. The city sprawled around its central point, a high domed spire that flashed gold in the rays of the sun. The spire led down to a fair grey castle, made of smooth marble, its windows glancing silver as light caught them.

Berev paused and gazed at it, the first sight of her kingdom for four centuries, though she said nothing and soon followed Loretta through the tall gates. They headed in the castle's direction. The city bustled with creatures of all sorts, such as Loretta had not seen before, but recognized from books she'd read in her Own World— rabbits in military uniforms with swords at their hips; satyrs and fauns, their hooves shod with gold, tripping down the cobblestone streets; tall, jeweled figures as beautiful and imperious as faeries. Songs rang through the city. Some were played on flutes, some were sung by young well-dressed women as they walked laughing down the streets—all were joyful.

As they neared the castle, the girls could see the sun blazing large and vibrant above it, looking so near that Loretta thought if she could climb onto the gold spire she could reach up and warm her hands upon it the way you warm your hands at a fire. The satyr guards standing at the castle gates glanced over the girls, their eyes lingering on Berev for a moment. "Who wishes to enter the castle?"

"I am Queen Berev, released from my curse in the west after many centuries," the girl-Queen declared, holding up the gold thread that had bound her. The guards inspected it, muttered together, and then waved them in silently. Loretta hesitated briefly, but Berev strode through and Loretta followed her into a courtyard—a wide open area completely taken over by flowers and trees, wild and untamed, like a meadow surrounded by distant walls. The girls wandered through and to the door set directly under the golden spire, and there were guards there, too, who let them through once they had seen the thread.

The room they entered was long and narrow, but the roof soared high above them and stained-glass windows let in rainbows of light. Slender grey pillars emblazoned with stars supported the roof, and the walls were hung with tapestries as far as Loretta could see.

The tapestries shone with rich colors in the light of the windows, and as Loretta walked down the hall they told a great history that she had no chance of understanding in whole, except that there had been great kings; crowns of silver; hunting parties; and fair women riding huge horses with gleeful laughs; but there were also huge towers; voids of black; twisting trees with branches like claws; stony, bleak moorland; men with fatal wounds; and women crying over piles of bodies. It was, Loretta found herself thinking, as if the tapestries were showing every wonderful story that had ever been written or thought or told.

Halfway down the hall, Loretta realized the shape at the end was in fact a throne, and on the throne sat a King, a young man, lithe and handsome and cloaked in green and purple. He stood to greet them as they approached, and he was reassuringly human, unlike the satyrs guarding his castle.

"Fine greetings to the past ruler of Kingsmere. Through the centuries, your family, of whom I am the latest, has passed down the tale of your curse. As King of Kingsmere, I formally apologize for my ancestor's actions. It was a quite unacceptable method of solving disagreements."

"You are the King?" Berev raised her chin to look the man in the eye. Loretta felt suddenly very out of her depth; never before had she imagined what might happen when she arrived with the former ruler to seek help from the current.

"I am. Rest assured, you shall be held in reverence and given all you require and wish for, out of respect for your past rule. But I would advise against an attempt to take your former place on the throne—and so would many of my subjects, I believe."

Berev was quiet for a long moment. "I noticed many things in this city as we passed that were not there when I ruled: less markets and more theatres. Satyrs and faeries, which would never have dared venture from their forests in my time."

"Your time was great, in its way," the King said gently. "However, it was not Berev of Kingsmere that built up the wealth and prosperity of this kingdom so long ago, but your mother and father, and their mothers and fathers. My family has passed down the tale of your rule, but probably from a very different perspective than you remember. It was a time of great trade, but little joy. Did you not hear the songs in the street as you walked?"

"Yes, I did." Berev turned to one of the windows and stood there, staring down at the city sprawled beneath them. "Do you swear that you have done better than I?" she asked finally.

"I have done all in my power to do better than you, Berev, as your cousin swore when she took your throne. Though, you will never see me curse my enemies and send them to while out centuries alone."

Berev nodded and turned back. "Then I will accept you as King, and I will take a place as a courtier in your house. I give up all claim to your throne. I hope that you would allow me to learn from you, and you from me."

"I will welcome your advice, and I will give you whatever knowledge you seek. Now that we are settled on matters of politics, I will turn attention to the stranger in my court." The King called for chairs from a servant standing by. "Come. Sit and tell me how curses were broken, and why one of you wears not the clothes of This World but of Another."

They did so, Berev regaling him with tales of her ruined castle and her friendship with Loretta which had been forged by song and in the darkness of a dragon's lair, and then Loretta told him of her quest for something to bring home, she thought there was something about the King that reminded her of the Keeper in the House. Once she had finished, he turned to her.

"You showed friendship to a lonely girl even when your quest was dire, and you have been brave on your quest to save your World. For that you shall be rewarded and helped, for I believe Kingsmere has the very thing you need to help your people. If you and Berev would follow me?"

The King stood from his chair and led Loretta and Berev by their hands out of the hall and further into the castle, weaving through wide and narrow passages. They came to a large room, upon the walls of which hung countless spools of thread. Berev, with a smile, laughed and handed Loretta a basket, her eyes bright.

"Of course! The same thread which was used to imprison me is just as powerful when used for any other purpose."

"Take what you want," the King said. "You have come for something which you cannot find in your own world, full of theories and dread and slow on action and hope. Here we have the thread of Kingsmere, renowned in this World for the enchantments which it places upon anything. With this thread, you can take the darkness of Night and turn it into something beautiful, not endless shadow but shade in sunlight."

Loretta filled her basket with all manner of thread, some of it as thin as the gossamer of spiderwebs, others as thick as one of Berev's braids. Most wondrous of all was the colors—there were all types of colors and shades, many of which she had never seen before.

They left the thread-room and came to a courtyard, much like that which they had passed through earlier except that it held a grove of trees, sheathed in ebony bark and sprouting ivory leaves. In the center of the grove stood a House, grand and royal and topped with gold like the King's castle. And in the center was a Door, just as that which Loretta had opened so long ago in her Own World. The King held it open, and the inside was just as she remembered: the same kitchen, the same staircase trailing in a long lazy spiral up and through the roof, the same hallway stretching out far, far before them.

The King went into the hallway and stood before the first door on the right. "This is your World," he told Loretta. Loretta pulled open the door and looked out into that smokey dim greyness

73

which she'd nearly forgotten in the freshness of That World. Something in her heart quailed at the thought of leaving this beautiful place, even with her basket of enchanted yarn.

Berev smiled at her, then embraced her quickly. "Go through, and sew something beautiful from the threads of the Night." The King looked like a ruler of old stories, and Berev looked gay and adventurous, and as Loretta looked back at Berev, standing in the threshold of the door to her World, she felt as though their souls would recognize the other's instantly if they ever were to cross paths again. The thought strengthening her, she stepped through the door and heard it close behind her.

Loretta stood in the forest outside the house, somewhere in Virginia again, and she could hardly see through the smokey grey. Still, she peered up until a lance of silver met her eye and she exclaimed in relief and exaltation. "The star! It is still there!" It was the only one in the sky, but the moon was bright.

She made her way back through the forest and to her home. Her parents, weary as they were, rushed out the door and embraced her tightly, babbling about how many days it had been, and that they had seen no sign of her in the forest or the town, and that with heavy hearts they had given her up for dead.

Loretta went to the chair where she had done so much knitting. She took up her knitting needles, and opened her basket of yarn from Kingsmere. The bright colors shone with a light so bright and radiant she thought it must be the light of the sun from the Other World. She unraveled a thread, set it around her needle, cast her first row, and turned to the window.

The dark Night whirled outside, as terrifying as ever, but now, as she knit, the spools of thread shone, and the Night broke up into its own individual threads. It floated through the sky, through her window, and into the rows of stitches, adding a deep grey-silver cast to her yarn but not darkening the color or the light of the Other World's sun. It was wholly unlike the way in which it had cast its shadow over her projects before; now it seemed as though the shadow was an indistinguishable part of the whole image, swallowed up by the vibrancy and only recognizable when one peered with the express intention of finding it.

It took many days to stitch the Night into her project, and as the days passed and the Night flowed into her window and was swallowed up, the journalists and academicians and scientists came in droves to their door, until her parents could barely step outside to pick the tobacco leaves. Through the chattering and the questions, Loretta continued to quietly knit, focusing on the picture forming in the yarn under her hands.

After a week, once the journalists and academicians and scientists had given up hope of getting their answers, the threads of Night still hanging in the sky cleared entirely, knit into the shadow of an orange tree.

Loretta stood, and the questions and chattering ceased. She rolled out a bright-colored blanket; set into its middle was the Keeper's House, and the girl-Queen's bier, and the dragon's cave full of treasures, and Virginia's rolling mountains outside her window, and around all of this twined a border of thick, darkly-shaded leaves and fruits and berries and vines. Over it all hung the gold thread of the sun.

The blanket became an heirloom, and many decades later, after Loretta had died and the world had changed once again and the tale of the Night had become just that, the blanket was hung in a museum—donated by some anonymous man of whom the only thing anyone could remember was that he had looked kingly and had smelled of sunlight and fresh growing things. There it became a remarked-upon work of art, something from ages past that could be touched and felt and marveled at.

The Summons

The Boy in the Castle

By Evelyn M. Lewis

Chapter One

It was a perfectly ordinary day for Ilya Severin.

His attacker, a bulky brute with tattoos and tanned skin, brandished half of a beer bottle threateningly. Ilya picked up a chair and held it in front of himself, four legs outward for defense.

"Watch who you mess with next time, bilge scum!" the man bellowed. He grabbed the legs of the chair and wrenched it sideways, swinging the bilge scum with it.

Ilya slammed bodily into the wall, and crumpled to the floor, clutching his stomach. He didn't bother to get up, but waited for the man to leave.

After the pub had settled down, Dimitri came over and found him. The younger man crouched down. "What happened this time?" he asked in a low voice, looking over his shoulder to make sure everybody was back to minding their own business.

"He called me a coward and a weakling."

"So you decided to prove him wrong, did you?"

"Gave him a good sock in the jaw." Ilya accepted Dimitri's offer of a white napkin, and wiped the blood dribbling from his nose.

"I can't leave you alone for half a day, can I? You're already drunk."

"I come to the bar to find work," said Ilya.

"Work? You're not even sober."

"What of it?" Ilya coughed, and pulled himself into a sitting position.

"You're supposed to be the best smuggler in Rostek."

"I am the best smuggler in Rostek." He gave a crooked grin.

"Oh? How will I present you to your client in a state like this?"

Ilya rubbed his nose gingerly. "My client?"

"Yes, your client. I decide to pay back that favor and get you a job, and this is what you give me to work with? Come on, let's get you back to the inn."

Ilya splashed his face with water and then rinsed out his greasy, shoulder-length hair in a wooden bucket. Finally he dried off his face with a towel, and with it came the last traces of the blood and grime.

"I need a drink…"

"No," said Dimitri, standing behind him.

"Of water. Relax."

"Behind you." Dimitri pointed to a copper cup on the vanity.

He turned around in the inn's washroom, found the cup, and sipped it slowly. Then he sat on a wooden stool and started to comb through his hair. "So, you say that you no longer owe me a favor. What have you come up with?"

"Last night a noblewoman, one of those landed gentry, it would seem, sent her servant to the pub. He said his mistress would hire only the best smuggler in Rostek. It had a well-paying sound to it, so I mentioned your name."

"I see. Well then, fine. Count it even. When is my appointment?"

"Half past eleven tomorrow."

"Did she happen to give a name?"

"No." Dimitri shook his head. "She'll meet you at Saint Beska's Abbey."

The next morning, Ilya dressed in his best waistcoat and tie. He had brushed his hair and washed it with nothing classier than a bar of soap. He had bathed well enough to hopefully not stink, although it was hard to fully get rid of the smell of alcohol.

Dimitri met him downstairs in the front of the inn, and wrinkled his nose. "Perhaps some mint."

"No time." He waved off the young man, who had been hanging around him like some kind of gnat since they ran the last commission together. (He hated to admit it, but Dimitri's imagined debt to him was probably actually just pity for his sorry state.) "I'm running late." It was an hour's ride to the abbey. For the good smuggler, nothing was more important than punctuality.

"Good morrow, then." Dimitri gave a wave and retreated to the upstairs rooms.

Ilya went out back to the stable, saddled up, and started off to the Abbey.

Saint Beska's was outside the city of Rostek proper, to the north, but still within the bounds of the principality of Rostek, which was a small kingdom of the East.

The Abbey sat on a rolling green. There were hedgerows for two miles, finally giving way to trimmed topiary and then the walls of the spreading complex. This was a place for nuns; men did not usually come here, and he wondered if this woman, whoever she was (not a nun, certainly?) was planning to admit him.

When he rode up to the iron-studded gates, he dismounted and approached, wondering if a knock on such a large door would even be noticed.

But as it turned out, no knock was necessary, for there was a shout from above and the gates began to open. He stood back.

The woman came out alone. He understood as soon as he saw her why she had not come to the pub in person. She was in her fifties, and had on a black half-mourning dress, with a purple train. He could not see any jewelry, but mourning clothes could be deceptively simple, and the silk of her dress seemed to exude hidden wealth. She was not wearing a veil.

So then, a dowager noblewoman whose husband was recently deceased. But not too recently—within the past year or so.

"Madame," he said, and politely made a small bow.

"Sir." She did not smile. Nor did she seem terribly impressed. "I sent for a smuggler. Are you he?"

"Now ma'am," he said carefully, "All my trade business is of course perfectly lawful." These naive nobles lacked any sense of the rules of the game. He wasn't of a mind to incriminate himself before establishing a rapport.

"Then I have no use for you." She turned around and started to walk back toward the doors.

Ah— he was losing her. "Now, hang on just a moment."

The woman stopped walking.

"I am… very good at what I do."

"I sent for the *best* smuggler in Rostek," she said, looking back at him.

"I stay humble." He scratched at his collar.

Her eyes sharpened. "We may have business, then."

He nodded. Now they were on. "What do you need?"

He could hazard a guess. He had a burgeoning suspicion about who she was. A noble, yes, but not a noble of Rostek – she was from the kingdom of Belovia, toward the south, just like he was. An ongoing civil war there had dethroned the King, and as revolutionaries, called the Vroek Coalition, hunted down and killed the Belovian nobles, they had fled to surrounding countries. This woman had doubtless fled recently, and most likely had left behind some valuable or sentimental personal property that she wished for him to retrieve.

He smiled confidently.

"I wish you to escort me and my son into Belovia," she said.

Ilya took half a step back, stunned. It took him a moment to reply. "To a country fraught with war?"

She raised an eyebrow. "To the capital. Stosla."

"Surely you must have gone to great pains to escape from

The Summons

A Salt and
Light Anthology

82

there," he ventured.

She looked at him drily, and he thought her eye twinkled a bit, but he couldn't be sure. She wasn't going to say anything.

"You would be heading into great danger."

"I am aware of the risks."

"What are you going to do when you get there?"

"I have made arrangements."

Ilya thought about this. Perhaps she had a cover— and a safe house. She was a spy, perhaps. A spy for the royalist side of the conflict. If she knew what she was doing, this could work. But—

"How old is your son?" he asked. "He is nine years old."

"Nine?!" Ilya stepped back, setting his teeth into a grimace. He folded his arms, looking at the ground, and kicked a pebble. "What shall I call you, madame?"

"You may call me… Madame Olga," she said, as if deciding on the name.

"All right, listen, Madame Olga. I'll take you anywhere you wish to go, but this isn't any kind of journey for a child."

"He must come."

"With all due respect, Madame, it's madness to bring a child on a trip like this." His deferential mask was slipping, and he tried to put it back on, but it was a bit of a lost cause. "Children are…

unpredictable. He will be a liability. Such a journey calls for… discretion… and… fortitude. You should leave him here, where he's safe." A child of only nine years would certainly get them all killed.

Olga's lips tightened, but she remained unmoved. "He is non-negotiable."

He sighed, trying to imagine the journey and the accommodations. Ilya wiped a hand across his face. "Is he quiet?"

"My son is very well-mannered. Will you do it or not?"

"I'd like half up-front."

She smiled for the first time. "Done. It shall be paid on our next meeting. Come again this time tomorrow."

Ilya shook her hand, feeling sweaty

He started turning around back to his horse, then paused. "Expenses also upfront."

"Expenses?"

"I'll need coin to rent a stagecoach."

She reached into her purse. Ah, finally.

"Let the record show that I was against this," said Ilya, mostly to himself, as Madame Olga loaded her son Alexei into the back of the stagecoach.

He was sitting on the driver's board, behind the horses, out in the front. A nun lifted a large wooden chest into the carriage. That box would contain all of his passengers' personal effects.

In the coach, shrouded by curtains and wooden doors of diamond-shaped lattice, sat the boy, with a cage full of eight white doves on his lap. Tight accommodations, but the birds would just have to make do.

Madame Olga's coin had bought the stagecoach; the trip was too risky to rent one. He had plans to sell it for a little extra money if he could get it back over the border after the trip. They were in need of two horses to pull the thing, one of which was his own and the other of which had been provided by Olga.

As for the upfront payment… it was burning a hole in his pocket already. His purse jingled and he eventually decided just to stuff it under the seat. There was no point in making themselves more of a target for highwaymen than they already were.

The first leg of the journey was not difficult. They set off after supper, and made it to the border around nightfall, as had been Ilya's intention, to avoid notice. They traveled on a back road. There was a swathe of farmland that cut across the two kingdoms' borders, with no marked boundaries save those of the farmers' properties. The carriage bounced and rattled on the dirt path, and he winced. The vehicle was going to lose half its value on this journey alone.

He drew them around carefully by a roundabout way to get back on the main roads by dawn. If they looked to be traveling east to west, rather than north to south, they could disguise where they'd come from, and appear less suspicious. For now, it didn't really matter that they were technically heading away from their destination.

In the late morning, they stopped at a Belovian inn near the border. When his passengers got out of the coach, the boy was rubbing his eyes, and Ilya could see that he had been asleep. The woman put her hand on his shoulder and steered him into the inn with her.

It was a small wooden building, painted white, with bright red cross-work in the current fashion. Within, there were few other guests. Those who were there evidently had little time to spare lingering downstairs.

The coach was stabled in the back, and Ilya worried about attracting attention with it, but there was no good alternative.

They slept in two rooms. In the early evening, Madame Olga paid the due, and they were off again. This time they were to travel for an extended period of time so as to get back on schedule. It would do no good to continue traveling at night.

During this stretch, Alexei slept in the back of the coach, but Ilya stayed awake at the reins. He didn't know if Olga was awake or only resting—she could mind herself.

When the sun rose and the day came again, he was struck, not for the first time, by the natural beauty of Belovia. The fields of golden wheat, the barley and the rye hadn't been visible at night, but now they waved joyously in the sun.

Later in the day, though, the landscape began to undergo an ominous change. Wide swathes of crops were blackened and burned. There were withered, stooped trees along the side of the road, and even the sky seemed darker. On the road they passed no one, except two entire wagons going the opposite direction, and the riders gave them wary glances.

When they finally got to the next inn at which he had planned to stop for the night, they were all thoroughly exhausted.

The inn was completely deserted, and this time they were the only guests.

"Where are you coming from?" asked the innkeeper after they paid. Perhaps he suspected them of something, but he sounded mostly incredulous to see them.

"We're traveling from Stosla to Rostek," he said.

The innkeeper gave him a dry glance, likely suspecting that they were nobles trying to flee the country. It was all right for people to be suspicious, thought Ilya, as long as nobody suspected the truth.

He might as well get more information while he could.

"When were they here?" he asked in a low voice.

"They?"

"You know."

"The Vroek Coalition passed through here two days ago and moved towards the south."

This was concerning to hear. When they got up to their rooms, he stopped Olga before they parted for the night. Alexei clung to her skirt.

"We need to talk."

When she looked surprised by his announcement, he knew this conversation wasn't going to be easy.

"Listen," he said. "The Coalition being this far east wasn't on my agenda. It's going to be hard to travel through this territory without being noticed."

"It was a possibility I was aware of," said the woman.

"Well, it wasn't a possibility *I* was aware of. And in case you haven't noticed, I have a neck too." Alexei stared on, wide-eyed, but Ilya paid him no mind.

"What are you going to do, then?" she asked him, placing a light hand on the boy's shoulder. "Leave us?" Her eyes were challenging, unblinking.

What *was* he going to do? Leave them?

He could.

On the other side of the hill, the marching men advanced. They crouched, with their backs to the rocks. The smell of gunpowder filled the air. Moonlight shone on their bayonets. He started to crawl away.

"Ilya! Where are you going?"

He steadied himself on the latch of the door. "What? No. I wouldn't— I wouldn't do that."

She didn't know, he reminded himself. She didn't.

"But," he reiterated sharply, "we can't continue on your preferred course. I can't take you all the way to Stosla with the situation as it is."

"We must make it to the Capitol," the woman insisted predictably.

"I know, I know. But things are much too unstable around the Capitol. You could wait—"

"No. Our mission is important. We must make haste."

It was the first time she had openly mentioned a mission. He pinched the bridge of his nose.

"Very well. We will go further east, and circle around these lowlands. We'll travel near the mountains, until we come toward the south side of the Capitol. Then I will deliver you to Lohova, which is only five miles from the Capitol. If you still want to go on from there, I'm sure you can figure it out," he added with some distaste.

"This will make us late by many days," said Olga.

"Nonetheless, it is the best I can do."

Olga gave a curt nod, indicating that she was willing to accept the compromise.

Chapter Three

The next day they set off eastward, in the direction of the mountains. It was a short and low-lying range for the most part, but the foothills jutted up against the plains here, creating a craggy, barren landscape that was nearly devoid of trees.

By mid-afternoon, they were rolling along a road that wound parallel to the mountains, through a rocky crevasse. It was bumpy, with stray sharp rocks lying about as if scattered by a careless hand.

When the carriage went over a particularly sharp one of these rocks, there was a loud *crack!* and he felt the carriage jolt. Ilya reined in the horses with some alarm.

The coach leaned. Olga was already pulling aside the curtain and looking out.

It was obvious to him at a glance that something was wrong with the wheel. But when he crouched down, he found that it wasn't broken, it had just popped off the wheel hub and become crooked.

"We've lost a hub," he said, "don't worry, I've got a spare under the seat," which was true, "and we'll be back on our way shortly."

He started back up to the driver's box, fully intending to lift it up and get the spare hub, when his senses suddenly pricked up.

They were in a ravine, passing between two high rock outcroppings. He could have sworn he'd heard a soft sound, coming from behind the rocks on the left. And the more he thought about it, the more certain he was that he'd heard the word, "wait."

If only he were wrong. But he wasn't wrong.

Without slowing down or giving any sign, Ilya circled in front of the horses around to the other side of the coach,.

On the right side of the carriage, he pulled open the curtain. Olga started, not having expected to see him again so soon. He held up a finger for silence and leaned in. He kept his voice low and his tone casual.

"Do not get out of the coach, and don't make any sudden moves. I believe we may have been ambushed."

Whatever happened to their wheel hadn't been an accident. It was not uncommon for highway robbers to create hazards on the road specifically to trap stagecoaches.

Olga's eyes widened. The boy looked at her questioningly.

"Ilya," she said, and it was the first time she'd used his given name. "Listen to me." Her eyes moved to the boy. "If they find him, they will kill him."

"Wh—" he started to ask, then realized there was no time for such questions. He nodded.

The woman pulled out the large wooden chest from under the seat and started throwing things out of it. Clothes, mostly, but he could see some other things in the bottom, such as papers and maps. "Alexei," she ordered the child, "get in the chest."

The child looked startled, but his mother's voice brooked no dispute.

Ilya backed away from the window, pushing the curtain shut, and took stock of their surroundings.

They had probably been followed, watched on the road for some time. There was nowhere to go, and even if he jumped on now and lashed the horses, the coach was liable to fall down, with the wheel askew. They were scuttled.

As if in reply to his thoughts, several men raised their heads over the edge of the rock. They had long-barreled flintlock muskets, tipped with sharp bayonets. But worst of all, their ragged green uniforms indicted that these were no ordinary highwaymen.

Apparently, he had the privilege of being ambushed by the Vroek Coalition itself.

He held on tightly to the reins of the horses as the group, which proved to be about ten strong, came down from behind the rock.

"Hands in the air," said one of them, perhaps their captain.

Ilya put his hands up, reflecting on how he'd chosen this route to avoid the Coalition in the first place, and now it was all for nothing. What were they doing this far east? There was nothing worth having out here. No cities, barely any population.

The leader smirked. "Well, well, well. What do we have here?"

"Ah, the usual. Just passing th—"

"Step away from the horses, please."

He took a step back.

A second man prodded the door of the coach with his bayonet, and then pounded on it hard enough to shake the carriage. "Come out of there!"

Madame Olga opened the door with some procedure, and stepped out, lifting her thick skirts. She frowned and gave the man a look down her nose.

A third man took the reins of the horses and hopped up on the driver's box.

"What's going on—" Ilya started.

The leader leveled the rifle at him. "We're taking everything with us. It's easier to just drive."

"You're going to have to fix the wheel first." Ilya smirked.

The men looked at each other, and then one of them said, "All right, as you were. Carry on with it, then."

Ilya pointed at the driver's seat, and the captain nodded. He lifted the seat and got out the wheel hub, fumbling in order to stall. When his coin purse was revealed, the rebels pounced on it without hesitation.

At this point they believed that he was traveling with just Olga in the coach. What was it that Olga said about the boy? *If they find him, they will kill him.*

So far, no one had searched the vehicle.

"Well, go on then," prodded the captain.

He gingerly returned the wheel to its proper place.

"Right." He and Madame Olga were herded together. "Walk."

They walked beside the stagecoach as it moved at a slow roll, one of the rebel soldiers at the fore. It was a forced march, but not a particularly long one. As soon as they got around the next bend in the mountain, he understood. This was no chance encounter with a band of rebels who had lost their way.

There was a great cave up ahead, high in a rocky peak, under a sheltering overhang. And perched in the mouth of the cave, in a wonderful, unassailable, hidden position, was an austere, utilitarian looking castle. It was certainly more of a military fortification than a summer residence, and doubtless very old. The walls were whitewashed, but unpainted, and the windows were dark and square.

There was a threadlike bridge leading from the place where they stood across a wide, perilous chasm to the castle. The coach stopped.

The captain of their little group hailed a guard on the other side, and someone started coming across to meet them.

"What is this place?" asked Ilya, tremulously.

"Welcome to Castle Tyrna," said the captain. "Headquarters of the Vroek Coalition."

Ah! The King's army had been searching all four corners of Belovia for months, and yet been unable to find these very headquarters. And now here they were.

It was precisely because he had gone out of his way to avoid trouble, that he had dragged them all straight into it. Ilya cursed his own stupidity. If only he had just stayed the course. To think he'd been attempting to drive a coach right past Castle Tyrna without being accosted.

Now two men opened the doors of the coach. There was no hope of the vehicle going across the bridge; whatever they were to loot had to be carried by hand.

The clothes and loose items were thrown into a basket. The case of pigeons came out, none too gently, and the birds rustled and clucked as they were handed off. The men lifted out the chest by the handles on each side.

He tore his eyes away.

Don't even look at the chest. Don't draw any attention to it.

For a moment, he caught Olga's eyes, and with a single glance he read the same thoughts. For the first (and perhaps the last) time, they were truly on the same page.

They walked across the bridge single-file. This was an amazingly well-defended position, he thought with some dismay.

They passed through the guard-house into the compact castle's small courtyard. The basket and the chest were thrown down with a painful thud. He winced, but the boy remained silent.

"Let's search them now," said one soldier. "She looks like one of those rich nobles. Can't wait to find out what they were doing out here."

Ilya tensed as the soldier reached toward the latch on the chest.

A man was hurrying down the steps from the keep. He was in his early twenties and had a shaven face and a clean uniform, unlike the other men.

"Hold on, now, wait," he said. "General Boris has not yet arrived."

"They're up to some devilry, Anatoliy," said the captain. "There's no good reason for a noblewoman to be in these mountains."

Anatoliy considered them with some interest. It was clear that he was more highly ranked than any of the others, but they did not seem to respect him yet. A new officer, perhaps. When his eyes fell upon Madame Olga, Ilya thought he saw a glimmer of recognition, but he couldn't be sure. If there was recognition, there was also deep confusion, and even… fear? But it was erased in a moment.

"If they are suspicious," said Anatoliy, "the General will want to examine their things himself, and he will not appreciate them being looted. Take the chest upstairs— to my quarters. I will guard it."

"Oh yes," he heard muttering behind him, "so you can have a gander at it I suppose."

"Watch your mouth," said Anatoliy. "General Boris placed me in charge in his absence, and I'll thank you to follow orders and stop this insubordination."

The soldiers all shuffled their feet.

"All right now, pick it up and move it." The men picked up the chest by the handles on each end. "The lady comes with me."

The soldiers prodded Olga, and she finally lowered her hands to pick up her skirts and follow Anatoliy up the steep stairs to the keep. She gave Ilya one last, unreadable look and then turned her back to him.

"What are you going to do with her?" he asked apprehensively.

"Oh, don't worry about it." The captain sneered. "Anatoliy is a civilized Christian man, he wouldn't hurt a lady."

"Nor a gentleman, I hope," added Ilya wistfully.

"You? A gentleman? Don't make me laugh."

Chapter Four

I do look a bit of a ruffian, Ilya thought ruefully, as the men chained his hands to the wall in the dungeon. What he wouldn't give for a drink right about now.

They had come through the interior of the castle— first the main hall, then the barracks. The interior parts of the castle were, oddly enough, less cramped than the outer parts, for the cave was quite spacious, while the ledge the castle was built upon was quite small.

There was a passage from the barracks to the dungeon. These were the castle's backmost parts, although where lay the true backmost part of this cavern was a mystery to perhaps anyone.

Simply put, it was a raw stone cave. Three sides of the prison were natural rock, and the ceiling was quite high. Through the gloom, he could see a few sharp-looking stalactites. The walls were rough and pockmarked, with holes leading off to probably nowhere.

The prospect of poking around and trying to find a passage to escape would have been irresistible if he hadn't been presently shackled to the wall. Which was probably why they had done that. The chains were not very long, and when he sat down on the ground, his hands floated near his head.

After the rebel soldiers had gone, he was alone, and Ilya promptly set about feeling sorry for himself.

Seeing as Anatoliy was presently focused on Madame Olga, he was at least momentarily forgotten. It was a small comfort to him that the man now in charge was supposedly a decent fellow. For all the difference that it made him. He was just the coachman, a disposable manservant. Perhaps they would forget him, and he would rot away down here.

After he had been carrying on in this glum state for several hours, there was a rustle at the far end of the cave. Ilya squinted into the gloom.

Something was moving back there. He jolted, shrinking back, breathing fast. A hundred thoughts ran through his mind, each more far-fetched than the last. There was some dog or wolf, kept in here to kill him. This had been his death sentence all along and he hadn't known. It was a cave beast, a monster, or a demon.

"H… hello?" he called out shakily. "Who's there?"

A small figure emerged into the torchlight. It was only Alexei.

He seemed to almost gleam in the torchlight, especially his halo of wispy hair, not yet turned from a child's pale blond. He had changed from the clothes he had on earlier in the coach, and was now wearing his long white night-dress, which made him look like a curious ghost.

"Mister Ilya?" said the boy.

"How did you escape?" Ilya asked in disbelief.

The Summons

A Salt and
Light Anthology

102

"I didn't," said Alexei. "Anatoliy let me out of the box."

"Yes, but… I mean, he found you? How did you get here?"

Alexei crept around the sides of the room, touching every face of the rock with interest. "He locked me in his room. He said that he locked the door to stop the bad men from getting in, and he told me not to open the door. He will bring me food and things."

Ilya breathed a sigh of relief. Anatoliy, if not on their side, had enough mercy to hide a child from the rest of the Coalition. This was a shockingly good turn of events. "You should have done what he said," he started to scold.

"Don't worry, I didn't open the door," said Alexei brightly. "I found a secret tunnel behind a bookshelf."

"Ah, yes, of course," said Ilya, staring directly into the torch flame. "Naturally."

"There are a lot of passages in there," said Alexei. "It's very lucky I found the one that leads to you."

"Like what sort of passages? Do any of them lead out of here?"

"I don't know," said Alexei. "I would like to help you escape, and Mama as well. But I think the hole that I just came out of is too small for a grown-up like you to fit into."

The shred of hope that had been gathering inside of him promptly dissolved.

"Well…" he struggled not to curse. "That's too bad. Where is

Anatoliy's room?"

"It's straight above us, I think. It's on the end of the outer ramparts, up against the cave wall. That's how come there is a tunnel in the wall."

He seemed very intelligent for a child, Ilya thought, and well-spoken, which he wouldn't have known from how quiet the boy had been on the coach ride. He also seemed much less shy around strange adults than before, but Ilya supposed that to Alexei, having few friends in this place and many enemies, perhaps they were no longer strangers. Besides, it may have been that the shackles made even an adult such as himself much less intimidating.

He'd never had a wonderful connection to children. He wasn't really sure how to talk to them. But he didn't have many friends right now either, and really wouldn't mind the— no. He cuffed himself mentally. He must see sense.

"If you can't escape," said Ilya, "you need to go back up there."

"How come?" the boy tilted his head.

"How come? Because right now anybody could come through this door to the barracks right here and discover you. At least Anatoliy doesn't want to hurt you. Go back upstairs."

Alexei looked a little hurt. "Fine, I… but…" he started backing toward the corner of the cave. "Fine, I'll see you later, Mister Ilya."

"Very well, yes, you can come back later. Now go." Alexei

shrank into a shadow and disappeared.

Ilya sighed and pressed his head against the wall. Now why had he told the boy he could come back later? And why was later better than now? Foolishness on his part. Selfishness. Alexei should not be here, he could be killed. As a matter of fact, Alexei and Olga both were in terrible danger, notwithstanding that they were upstairs and he was down here. She was the royalist spy, not him. The boy clearly didn't understand his own position, nor that of his mother, or he would be much more frightened.

Yet, how remarkable that there was a passage. Surely they could use this to their advantage. There must be a way to get messages to Olga— well, realistically, messages *from* Olga. Perhaps it wasn't such a bad idea after all. He would wait for the boy to return.

The Boy in the Castle

105

That morning, Anatoliy had visited Ilya for the first time since his capture. The acting-commander of the fortress finally came down to check on his prisoner, and Ilya felt immense gratitude when the man ordered the chains to be lengthened enough for him to freely sit, stand, and move about a little. Taking them off simply wasn't an option when the tunnels were every which way, he understood, but it was nice to be more comfortable, and Anatoliy had ordered some fresh straw, and then it was rye bread, which was dry, but sufficient at least. He still wished they would have given him a bedroom like Olga, but things were looking up.

Just after he finished eating, Alexei popped out quickly enough to startle him.

"Guess what?" the boy asked.

Ilya jumped, then went blank. "Guess…" he blinked.

True, it was not safe for the boy to be about. But at least the guards would probably not be coming back for a while, seeing as they had just gone.

"I've seen Mama!"

This was better news than expected. "You have?"

"Yes, sir! Anatoliy let her visit me for a bit."

"Has she told them anything?" Ilya asked, almost as curious to know for what mission he was rotting away in a Coalition dungeon as the Coalition was.

"She's trying to help you," said Alexei. "She told them that you're only a hired driver."

That was true enough. He got the sense that Olga was doing politics upstairs, furiously negotiating.

He couldn't see how this would end well for any of them. Olga would soon be proven a spy. Her papers had been captured along with her, and Anatoliy could only withhold them from examination until his superior came along, at which point a judgment would be made. If Olga was found to be a spy, that was the end for her, and likely him as well, assuming none of them were wanted for information, which was even worse. And then what would happen to Alexei?

"That's good," he said. He had no desire to talk about death and such unpleasant things, not in front of the child. There was no point in worrying him with any of that.

"What's going to happen to you, sir?" Alexei asked, approaching with some concern.

"To me?"

The boy must have seen the worry on his face. Ilya was momentarily at a loss. "I… I don't know."

Alexei looked troubled.

"Now, stop it," he said. "I don't want you worrying about me.

I'm grown up, I can take care of myself."

"I'm almost grown up too. Mama says I'm almost grown up."

"Ha!" Ilya laughed out loud.

The boy took a few steps backward, a look of hurt in his eyes.

"You're a child."

"A child," Alexei repeated.

"Aye."

"You don't like me, do you?"

"What? I didn't say that."

"You said it like it's bad. And yesterday you sent me away."

He made a wry face. "Well…" Was it he who had never liked children, or children who had never liked him? The children knew who he was, somehow. The boys stood in the vacant lot and threw rocks at him when he walked by, shouting names.

But if Alexei was judging him for anything, he didn't show it. He was too young, anyway, younger than those boys.

Alexei had already started to retreat off toward the corner, the one with the secret tunnel.

Ilya half stood up and then sat back down. "No, no, it's all right. I do like you. I'm sorry."

Alexei seemed uncertain.

He could comprehend how pathetic and desperate for human company he must be right now, as he knew it wasn't for the child, but for himself that he patted the rock beside him. "Please, don't leave. Come on, sit down."

Slowly Alexei came back over. He sat down cross-legged a safe distance away, just beyond where Ilya could reach with the chains. He seemed almost glum, though, and started to play with the little rocks on the floor.

"You know I only sent you away because I worry the soldiers will come in here."

Alexei looked at the door, and then back at the ground.

"You have to promise that if you ever hear something at the door, you will go back into your tunnel right away. And if I ever tell you to go, you must go immediately."

The child looked at the door, back at Ilya, then back at the door. "I think I can do that."

"Good." Now his conscience was at least somewhat at ease.

"You don't want the bad men to catch me."

"No, I don't."

"What if they did? Am I safe upstairs?"

"Safer," said Ilya, trying to sound more confident than he felt.

"Anatoliy is helping you, and I'm sure that he will get you out of here as soon as he is able."

"And then what?"

Yes, of course, that was a natural question to ask, although he was surprised at the child's forethought.

"Go to the King," said Ilya. "I suppose. Well, ask your mother if you can, but I'd assume you must go to the King."

"That's—" Alexei crinkled his mouth.

"Well, I know he's very important and you might not get to see him personally, but you make sure and find somebody who works for him."

"But…" Alexei trailed off, and this time Ilya didn't interrupt him. Finally he said, "Why? Why go to him, I mean? What will he do?"

It was clear this question had been the result of some thought. Ilya wasn't sure how much the boy could understand or knew about the mission, but he tried. "Well, you're the King's people, aren't you?" he interrupted himself. "Don't answer that. I know that your mother serves him. He will protect you. He has a responsibility to his subjects."

"What responsibility?" asked Alexei with some apprehension.

"A king has to protect his subjects, you know. If he's a good king, anyway. He would definitely help you if you needed it."

"Would he save Mother, too?"

"Yes, I'm sure that he will," Ilya said, trying to be reassuring. "If he can." He didn't want to oversell it.

"I hope he can," said Alexei uncertainly. "And you, too."

Ilya didn't meet his eyes, but stared at the other wall. "Haha." He laughed drily. "I'm not so sure about me. But you, yes."

"What!" the boy scrambled closer to him. "Why not you?"

"Well, it's not like they'll let me go now that I know where their headquarters are." It was something he had been thinking about.

The boy's eyes widened. "You can't just give up, sir!"

Giving up. Aye, it was true. Perhaps he did give up too easily. Still…

"Well…" he argued. "I don't think that the King likes me very much."

"What?!" Alexei demanded again. "I thought you said he was good. Why wouldn't he like you?"

Ilya hunched his shoulders in embarrassment, having backed himself into a corner. "It's not that he's not good. He is. It's me who's not very good."

"Oh." The child sat back, seeming somewhat bewildered.

"What do you mean? You're not like the bad men upstairs, are you?" He tilted his head. "I don't think you are."

Ilya made a wry face. "I may have done some crimes."

"Like smuggling."

Ah, so the boy knew a little.

"Not just that. I'm a deserter from the King's Army."

"Oh." Alexei seemed nonplussed.

"So, as I said, he wouldn't like me very much."

Alexei put his chin up defiantly. "I think that if he met you then he would like you."

Ilya felt a smile break over his lips against his will. "Ha. That's very cute."

"I mean it, though."

"All right."

At that moment, the door handle rattled.

Alexei jumped away like a rabbit. Ilya's heart pounded, but he needn't have worried. The boy was invisible in a second. As the door swung open, he dropped his head, went limp, and tried to resume a dejected posture.

It was not Anatoliy this time. "Coachman," said the soldier, "prepare yourself. General Boris will arrive within two days."

Chapter Six

Two days.

For the rest of the day and that night, Ilya thought of nothing except Alexei and Olga, in the upstairs rooms. He slept fitfully.

The next morning after breakfast Alexei came down again. "Have you seen your mother?" Ilya asked him.

"No," said Alexei.

"Well, maybe tomorrow," he said, trying to sound hopeful.

The boy yawned. Then he came and huddled up on the ground near to Ilya, with his knees pulled up to his chest. His nose poked out over his arms. After a minute Ilya heard a sniff, and realized the child was crying.

He froze, not really sure how to react.

"There, there, now," he said awkwardly, and gave him a tiny pat on the back. "What's wrong?"

It was probably because the boy was missing his mother, he thought.

"I don't want you to die," sniffled Alexei.

"What!"

"I couldn't sleep all night. I was thinking about you, and how they're going to kill you when the General gets here."

Ilya blanched. Though he had avoided bringing up the possibility of danger to Alexei or his mother, it simply had not occurred to him that the boy might worry on his account. In fact, it was hard enough for him to imagine that anybody would worry on his account, but much less this boy whom he'd known for a few days at best.

"Now, whatever makes you think that?"

"Why, you said they weren't going to let you go, and… well…"

Ilya cursed himself, but silently, on the inside. Of course, the boy wasn't stupid.

"Now see here. I'll not have you suffer a bit on my behalf. I won't have it. You have enough problems of your own to worry about. Just focus on staying hidden and communicating with your mother."

"But your problems are worse. I can come and go as I please and I get nice food every day. You're all chained up down here… in the dark, and…" He sniffed.

O mercy. The boy really didn't know that his own position was equally bad, if not worse. Neither of them was free, and Alexei was liable to be killed as soon as the General arrived, if Anatoliy ceased being able to hide him, or worse, turned him over. But he did not want to frighten the boy.

"Now look here," he said again, "I will just have to be brave, and so will you."

Alexei looked up. "I'm trying… Mother always tells me stories about brave heroes and princes, and what they would do when things happen. She always tells me to behave like them. But I don't know what they would do right now, and, well, I can't go to see Mother."

He should say something. He knew that he had to say something. "Ah, yes. Brave heroes. Kings. Princes. Knights." Ilya searched his mind.

"They're all so strong and tough, and big and tall; I don't know how I could ever be like that."

Well, that makes two of us, then, thought Ilya, but he said, "That isn't what makes a person brave."

"Isn't it? I suppose that if a knight were in my position he would simply kill all of the bad men and get us all out of here," said Alexei.

"Your position?" Ilya coughed. "The position of being nine years old? I don't think any of them could do any more than you've done."

"You think?"

"Oh yes. Anyway," said Ilya, "you've already done a lot."

"I have?"

"Yes…" It was more honest than he'd intended. "Just by being you."

The boy didn't say anything, but he sniffled a bit, and Ilya could swear that instead of crying, he was laughing.

"Hm?" he asked, kindly, wanting to ruffle the boy's hair but not sure that he should. "What's so funny?"

"Nothing."

Well, maybe crying after all.

"Well, anyhow, the point is that anyone can be brave. It isn't about being big or strong, it is about doing the right thing, even if it is hard or if you are scared. Maybe little folks like you are even more brave than the rest of us because of that."

"Why are they doing this to us?" asked Alexei, unexpectedly. He turned his face to the side and looked Ilya directly in the eye. "Why are they fighting the war, I mean?"

"Hmm." He tilted his head back against the wall and tried to think about how to say it. "They are former nobles, like you, but… they were among the corrupt ones whom the old King sent into exile. They hated the King and wanted to overthrow him. That is why they killed him. And now they are trying to kill the new King, his son, too."

"Sir, why do they hate him?"

"Because…" How did you explain it to a child? "They want to

be in charge."

"Why do they want to be in charge?"

"They think leadership is about something you get. Power. Privileges. But it's not."

"What do you mean?" asked Alexei.

"It's about serving other people. A king has to think about other people before himself. And especially… well the normal people, like the late King did when he tossed out Vroek and the others. But let's not get into the politics of it. Let's just say that he has to do hard things when they need to be done." *Ah, what do I mean by talking like I understand these things? As if I would know anything about it.*

As he spoke, Alexei listened, very quiet and sober.

Why, thought Ilya, *I am no more than a hypocrite.*

How could he impart some kind of courage that he did not even possess? Or give advice that he could not himself follow?

Chapter Seven

General Boris arrived the next morning.

Ilya found it out when the soldier, called Sergey, came in that morning to bring him his bread and water.

Alexei did not appear that day.

Later, when Sergey came back for dinner, Ilya dared to ask a question.

"Is there any news from upstairs?" he ventured.

"Aye. You're in trouble, coachman. Boris got out the lady's paperwork. She's got the royal seal all over everything. She was bound for Stosla, so we know where you were going."

"Ah… what's going to happen to her?"

"She was executed this morning just before noon. The General beheaded her and threw her body over the wall into the chasm."

Somehow, though he'd anticipated it, the news still came like a cold shock. Ilya flinched. Poor woman. So that was the end of that feeble hope. He wondered if the boy knew. For a moment, then, he felt a stab of panic, wondering if the boy had been turned over among the documents that Anatoliy had surrendered, but quickly he reasoned that there had been no mention of the child. If they had discovered him, surely Sergey would have mentioned it.

Still, he wasn't sure what he could do to help the boy at this point. If Olga was dead, it surely wouldn't be long until he was next.

But nothing happened. After Sergey left him, he sat alone for the rest of the day, and into the night, in growing dread, shifting uncomfortably with a twisting feeling in his stomach. The next time anyone came, it could well be the time for his execution. Boris was only busy, had better things to do than worry about some coachman, and he was left to try and make his peace.

It was some time during the night that the boy appeared.

Ilya hadn't known that he'd been sleeping, but he startled awake to find the boy standing in front of him, illuminated a gold color in the orange glow of the flame.

"Alexei!" He clamped down on the volume of his voice, and hissed the word. "You shouldn't be here."

"I know." The boy's face was pale.

"You've got to— to find a way out of here. Go through the tunnels. If you ever did find a way to escape, do it now. If you didn't— try exploring at the back of this cave. There's got to be one that leads out of here." Before, the boy had at least had his mother in the castle to stick around for. Now there was no reason to stay. There was no reason to assume Anatoliy's protection was strong enough. It hadn't saved Olga.

"I want you to escape too. I'm going to help you escape." The boy's teeth were gritted, his face was set in the most determined expression Ilya had ever seen, despite the tears starting from his eyes.

"Please. Don't do anything dangerous."

The most important thing was that he found some way to protect the child. If there was anything useful still that he could do with his life, it might be that. If only he could think of something. The child was innocent, indeed better than he was, and more worth it.

"Don't worry," Alexei said. "I've already done it."

"What? What have you done?"

"The doves. I let them go."

He blinked in confusion.

"I got into the— the aviary. It's at the top of the tower… above Anatoliy's room. I didn't have to— to open the door, I j-just climbed out the window and… up."

Ilya's eyes widened, genuinely impressed.

"I grabbed onto the stones. They are all uneven up there. I found the white doves we brought and I released some of them. They will fly to the King's army straightaway. I had written a message telling them that we are captured by the rebels at Castle Tyrna. Then I climbed back down."

"Didn't anyone see you climbing on the outside?"

"I— I don't think so. It was early morning, before the sun came up."

Before the execution. Before he found out. Ilya felt pity for the boy, but he also felt almost a bit relieved. Was that truly his entire plan? It was a touching thought, and at least the boy had been successful.

"It is a miracle," said Ilya, "that you weren't apprehended." He paused, since the boy was already on the verge of tears. "It was very brave. And now the King's army will find out where we are."

Though they wouldn't come to the rescue. There wasn't enough time. Not for him. He would be killed before they arrived. But maybe for the boy, he thought, desperately.

"Don't try anything else like that. Just try to escape through the rock. Please."

He waited for an answer, but received none. "Please, just go now."

Alexei didn't move; just kept standing there. The silence surprised him for a moment, until he realized that it was a glazed look, a kind of stupor. The boy's eyes stared past him, into some distance beyond the walls of the cave. Perhaps his words hadn't even been heard.

Ilya did not repeat his instructions.

Slowly, the boy fell to his knees, and crawled toward him, beginning to weep with great, desperate sobs, until he had fully curled up into Ilya's side, and continued weeping. Ilya slowly, uncertainly put his arm around him, like he was afraid to crush the child. Eventually, however, he was forced to relax. Soon he would really have to send the boy away. There was no sense in letting him be discovered. But just for a moment, for this moment, he could be of some comfort.

The Summons

A Salt and
Light Anthology

Chapter Eight

"Get up," said Sergey the next day. It came with a light kick in the foot, just enough that Ilya sensed he was being touched with a ten-foot pole. Did he really look that dirty?

He sat up and pushed himself to his feet.

"Give me your hands."

Ah.

His manacles were promptly unclasped.

"Come upstairs," said the man.

And so finally, for the first time in four days, Ilya got up and walked through the passage leading through the stone to the barracks, and then out to the courtyard into the blessed sunlight, which almost blinded his eyes. The sky was a light overcast gray. Then, finally, they ascended the stone steps up to the keep, and into the main hall.

The hall was whitewashed and mostly bare, except for the oaken table down the center, with two wood benches. Some green flags of the Coalition had been hung up on the far wall.

Boris was sitting at the head of the table. It was obvious who he was; his uniform was deep green with two rows of gold buttons, and he had a sword at his side in a gilded sheath. His hair was short and gray. He was bent over to one side, engaged in fervent conversation with an aide. There was a map on the table in front of them.

"Now you see. The King's army is stationed thusly." He knocked a piece against the table. "We are here." He jabbed a finger into another spot in the map, where soft lumps indicated mountains. "Now—"

He looked up abruptly. "Sergey."

"Sir."

Boris pushed back the wooden chair that he was sitting in and came to meet them.

"This is he?"

"Yes, sir."

"What is your name, coachman?"

"It is—" he felt momentarily tongue-tied. "It is Ilya, sir."

"Well, then, Ilya. My rear guard has arrived at the castle, and they bring a strange tiding. At the inn through which you last passed— the only inn presently doing business for twenty miles in every direction— the innkeeper told my men that you were a party of three."

The words sank into his bones with a chill.

"What?" Ilya exclaimed immediately, in feigned surprise.

"That can't be right." Lies were his bread and butter; they were automatic and effortless by now, and he was glad.

"Pavel!"

A small man stood up from the right side of the table. "Sir?"

"Tell him what you told me."

"Y-yes, sir…" the man stammered nervously, "the innkeeper said the last group had gone toward the mountains. 'All three of them,' he said, sir."

"It can't have been us," said Ilya. He kept the confident tone, but he knew that the fear was showing in his eyes by the way that the General smiled. "It must have been somebody else."

"This road leads nowhere but here. Do you really think another party could have passed by the castle on this road without my men knowing about it?"

The question was unanswerable, of course. He held his tongue and looked at the ground.

"Do you think? Answer me, wretch." The General slapped him loudly on the cheek with a backhand.

Ilya stumbled back a step. "I— I don't think."

"No you don't, you fool. What happened to the third person?"

"There wasn't any third person. Sir."

Boris slapped him on the other cheek. "Who was he? What sort of man was with you? Tell me now."

"Sir. I swear to you that I am telling the truth. There was no one else. Please believe me. It was Olga and myself alone. Sir."

Boris considered him for a minute with some disdain. "Sergey, take him back down to the prison. He must wait for my convenience."

"Yes, Sir."

Ilya waited alone with a growing sense of dread.

Was it not ironic that he had never had any actual loyalty to the King? He had betrayed the King by deserting his army, and his service to Olga had been purely mercenary; services offered to the highest bidder.

Yet now, he was going to be killed, and likely suffer quite a bit beforehand, and why? For the King's cause? Not at all, he knew nothing about Olga or her mission, it was a mystery to him.

No, but for the child, and him alone, personally. Naught else was of importance any longer.

It was a painfully long hour and a half before the General came down. Each minute seemed like an age. Ilya was grateful that Alexei did not appear again. Perhaps he had found an escape route after all.

The door creaked open, and he started to his feet, his heart pounding erratically.

Boris came in with Sergey and took an unimpressed look around.

"Your only prisoner at this time?" he asked his subordinate.

"Yes, sir."

"And what have you? The rack? The horse?"

Ilya blanched; he felt that his knees could no longer hold him and he sat down again quickly.

"If I may, sir," said Sergey. "A hundred copper coins, sir, may resolve this problem efficiently."

"You are a fool," said the General, "if you mean to let him go. He will make straight for the King's army and expose us. This man is an enemy to the glorious cause."

"No, Sir. We can't let him go. But we can let him live, sir, until such a time as may be more convenient."

Boris tilted his chin. "What say you, rogue?"

Ilya hesitated, feeling something grow within himself. He raised his eyes. An unfamiliar feeling burned hot inside of him— was this courage? He wasn't sure. It was at least defiance, or perhaps simply righteous indignation. He spat on the General's shoes. "I'll not have your money."

The General's eyes flashed. "So be it." His hand went to the hilt of his sword.

Now he'd really done it. Ilya squeezed his eyes shut, feeling nauseated.

"Wait."

There was a small voice. A faint voice, barely more than a whisper.

He opened his eyes.

They were all turned around. The boy stood behind them, dressed in his white night-dress. The cave was filled with a strange silence upon silence, as though a ghost had appeared in their midst.

Ilya was seized with horror.

"Who are you?" asked Boris at last. "How did you get in here?"

"It is me," Alexei said, in a quiet voice.

"O please, God, no," moaned Ilya. "Alexei, no. What are you doing?" But he trailed off when they glanced back at him, and he was far too shocked to continue.

"You!" General Boris exclaimed. "Is that your name?"

"Yes, it is."

A strange look came over the General's face.

"Now let him go, please." The boy's eyes were fixed on the leader of the Coalition unflinchingly, unremittingly, and the words were spoken in a commanding tone. Ilya felt the balance of power in the room had shifted, and had somehow become a negotiation between equals.

"You heard me, boy," argued Boris. "How can I let him go?"

"Because the King's army already knows where you are. They are on their way here already."

"You lie," said Boris.

"No." A smile twitched at the corner of the boy's lips. "If you go up to the tower where the birds are kept, you'll see. Find the birds that came in with us. You will find that I've released six of them. And the last two bear the message that I sent."

The General turned his head. "Sergey," he said, "go look."

"Yes, Sir." The man nodded and rushed out of the room as though he couldn't bear to be there a moment longer. There was a peculiar pressure building up in the air.

How long had the boy been planning this? To think—that long! And never a word? Outsmarted by a nine-year-old. And he thought he was clever.

Outdone by a nine-year-old. Undone by a nine-year-old. Unravelled. Ilya was somehow still on his hands and knees. Tears were dripping from his eyelashes. "You can't do this," he started again. "You're not… I'm… That's not how this is supposed to go. That's not how this works."

Alexei's wide blue eyes glistened, but he kept standing there.

Sergey returned, red in the face, huffing and puffing. He looked supremely bewildered. "Sir. It is as he says."

"Where were you?" asked Boris, tilting his head again and leaning on his sword inquiringly as he stared at the boy. "How did you get in here?"

But it was as though he was talking to himself, for he required no response. "You were in that chest, weren't you. The half- empty one, with the papers."

He stood up straight, suddenly, and put his sword back in the sheath. "He was in Anatoliy's room, wasn't he. Sergey! Fetch Anatoliy immediately."

"I…" Sergey twisted his hands, sweating. "I was afraid you would ask that, sir. Anatoliy hasn't been seen all morning, sir."

"What?!"

"He's nowhere to be found, sir."

"Has he run away in fear? Good riddance! And let that royalist traitor never return." Boris sneered in disgust. "Right under my nose, he was, and I let him have command of this base." He shook his head. Then, he looked up, as if just noticing that Ilya was still there. "Get him out of here."

"What?" Ilya scrambled to his feet.

"He is nothing but a common hireling."

"Sir?" questioned Sergey. "I thought you said…"

"What do I care about that? We have already won. Get him out of here."

Ilya stood as though dumbstruck while Sergey seized his wrists and unlocked the manacles. "And the boy, sir?" asked the soldier.

"He dies before nightfall."

"NO!" Upon hearing this, Ilya made a sudden and desperate move. He got as far as one hand in Sergey's face before an iron fist sucker-punched him in the stomach. He doubled over, the edges of his vision going gray. "No," he gasped. "Alexei, no. You can't," he mumbled as Sergey dragged him out. "No, you can't do this."

The last thing he saw before the door shut on the dungeon was the face of Alexei, wide-eyed and silent as the irons tightened around his wrists.

Ilya banged on the heavy oak outer doors of the guard-house, and his weak fists produced only a solid thudding sound. "Come on!" He yelled up at the battlements. "Let him go. He's just a boy. Please."

The men on the walltop scratched their heads and looked down at him.

"SIR, PLEASE!"

"Go away, man!" shouted the guard on top of the gate.

"What do you even want with him?!"

"How should I know? Get out of here! You should be grateful, you lout!"

It was only when one of them raised his crossbow that Ilya started to back across the threadlike bridge.

His horse was waiting on the other side. Yes, it was his horse. He eyed up the castle desperately. "You can't do this," he kept muttering to himself; a useless mantra. "You can't… you can't…"

He mounted the horse, and spurred it down the road in his frustration, then stopped, and reined it in. No, he couldn't—!

He pulled around and started awkwardly back in the other direction. There was the bridge again, but nothing was different. He rode back and forth aimlessly, back up and down the road, wandering, then stopping, as though sizing up the castle to attack it. He knew they were all watching him with amusement. Pointing and laughing, most likely. But what could he do? Boris had said it, he was only a common hireling, no threat whatsoever.

He continued this restless motion with increasing desperation throughout the day, as the sun fell lower in the sky.

Finally, when the sun was touching the far horizon in the west, he stopped and simply looked up at the castle from a distance. Everything seemed still and quiet. There was no motion, not even a breath of air.

The sun dropped below the horizon, and shadows fell across the land.

Now it was too late. Ilya slumped forward in the saddle. Not caring anymore, he dropped the rein and let the horse decide where to go.

The animal took him south, along the road toward Lohova. When he reached the town, it was still night. He paid no mind to his surroundings. But when he practically fell off the horse behind the first inn he encountered, something slid out of the saddlebag. It was his own coin purse. He opened it.

It was those accursed 100 coins.

Now it seemed only cruel to send them. He had half a mind to throw them in the gutter. But he had given no thought to how he was to pay for his stay.

After paying at the inn several days in advance, he set about trying to forget the events of the past week. This was mostly unsuccessful.

It was while he was there on the second day, drinking himself blind, that he felt a hand grab him by the back of the shirt.

"Well, if it isn't Ilya Severin."

He looked up to see the face of his old royal army captain.

Another glance around the tavern showed him what he'd been too drunk and dispirited to realize before. There were quite a few royal soldiers in here, actually, seated here and there, filling up the back tables, and they looked like they were celebrating.

All at once, everything that he'd seen while riding in, but not really looked at, clicked into place. The unusual numbers of people in the street. The colorful flags and banners hung from windows. The white doves flying in great flocks through the air.

This meant Lohova was controlled. And if Lohova was controlled, Stosla, the capitol, was controlled, and if the capitol was controlled…

Did we win?

"Well?" mocked the captain. "Too drunk to answer me? Do you regret leaving us, coward? You yellow-bellied, chicken-faced, lump of worthless—" He shook Ilya by the shoulders. "What's the matter? Aren't you going to defend yourself?" He dropped him in disgust, and Ilya sank back into the chair, limp and bleary. "Oh, that's right. You haven't got any *fight* in you, have you?"

"Oh come on," called another soldier across the tavern. "We're having a good time, my man. Just arrest him and have done with it."

"I suppose," the captain begrudgingly admitted to the soldier, his lieutenant.

"We can send him on to Stosla where they imprison the deserters. I heard the King is on his way there, to arrive soon."

"His arrival was delayed, no one knows where he is."

"Regardless, we took the city on his order, did we not? I'm sure he will be back on the throne soon. After we return from smoking out the Vroek Coalition's mountain hideout, you could even stop in to see soldier Severin sentenced, if you like."

"All right," grumbled the captain, although Ilya was sure he would have liked to beat the tar out of him on the spot.

Not even the news that the Vroek Coalition would soon be defeated could lift his spirits. The prospect of going straight back to jail, however, was darkly ironic.

And so, Ilya was taken to the Capitol at Stosla, and put into the royal jail. Now he had been imprisoned by both sides of the conflict in the space of a few days. But this time, it was for actual crimes. And he almost didn't care anymore.

At least, he told himself he didn't. But there was a small, barred window high in the wall, that looked out on the street level, and he found himself raising his head to look when the sound of marching feet passed by. After the space of one week, the boots of the King's men marched back through the streets. They had returned.

It was not long then before a man came to get him. It was one of the palace guards. This imprisonment had somehow gone much quicker than the last one, as though he had been half sleeping the entire time.

"You've been summoned by the King," said the guard.

Now, suddenly, he was fully awake, and painfully self-conscious. He started in alarm. "What?!"

"The King has returned and he asked for you specifically. By name. Come on."

Ilya shrank back, his eyes widening. He hadn't figured it was possible for things to get worse, but somehow they had. Most people were not sentenced before the King.

"Y…you've got the wrong idea," he stuttered. He didn't know what to say. Were they going to accuse him of some even worse crime than desertion, like treason? God forbid it had something to do with Castle Tyrna.

"I don't know what idea I've got," said the man bemusedly.

"The King wants to see you, that's all I know."

Still he hesitated. "What, right now?" he pulled at his clothes. "Like this?"

The soldier looked him over with a skeptical eye, seeing his dirt and sweat and grime. "No, not like that. We'll have you put some real clothes on."

The castle at Stosla was tall and white, with red colored rooftops. They walked through a great green courtyard with bushes pruned into elaborate shapes. There was a flock of white doves, kept by the crown, housed in one of the towers, and the flock was out, making joyous circles over the rooftops as domesticated birds are wont to do.

He could hear the sound of bells ringing across the lawn, up from the city outside. As they came toward the gilded doors, the doves swooped straight down the pavilion and flew up from behind them in a great cloud, so that he could almost feel the brush of their wings on his shoulders.

The doors opened. Sunlight slanted into the great hall through the upper windows, in bright golden beams. White flowers dripped from the windows and vases and every surface. Gold trimmed arches ringed overhead.

There were so many people.

It was actually only two dozen attendants or less, but to Ilya it seemed that it was many, and he felt overwhelmed. The men at the door were armed with swords. The women… why were there women?

From the other side, the King walked in. He was dressed all in red, with a long robe that dragged against the floor. On his head was a golden crown set with rubies.

A heralder announced him. "His Royal Majesty, Aleksandr II Konstantin."

Everyone in the room briefly kneeled. Ilya dropped to his knees, feeling like the breath was knocked out of his body.

Alexei ran up and threw his arms around him.

Suddenly, it was like a cloud passed out of his mind. He wasn't going to die, but it was more than that. He felt very alive. The colors in everything suddenly seemed sharper and clearer. Maybe it was all right, being alive.

"It's you," he said.

"It's me," said Alexei. They had partly separated but the boy held his hands with his small hands, and Ilya looked at them in wonder.

"But…" He looked around at the room full of people, more perplexed than anything, and sat back on his heels. "I… I don't know anything about anything, do I?"

Alexei gave a wan smile, but his eyes were full of tears.

"How did you survive?"

"Anatoliy helped me escape."

"I'm so confused. I don't understand."

"I can explain." A man's voice came from behind him, and he looked to see Anatoliy coming up behind. Now, instead of being dressed in the clothes of the Vroek Coalition, he was dressed in the Royal uniform. The young man bowed respectfully and smiled. "If you would permit me, Your Majesty."

"Yes," Alexei nodded. "Please."

"After the Queen and young Aleksandr fled Belovia, they stayed in secret at Saint Beska's Abbey in Rostek, hidden by the nuns. But the Queen knew that they would eventually have to return. From the abbey she sent communications with the army, and finally as the conditions grew more favorable, they signaled her, alerting her that they would within days retake Stosla, and that she and her son must return with all haste. For it is not good for a kingdom to be without a king.

"But, though their insider knowledge, which I had been providing for some time, told them that the Coalition was not likely to interrupt them on their planned route, the way was still through Coalition territory, and it was necessary to travel undercover and exercise the utmost caution. With them, they carried the royal messenger doves to signal their approach and order the army to advance into place to secure their position as they entered the city.

"As a spy infiltrating the ranks of the Coalition, I had been recently stationed in the headquarters at Castle Tyrna, but had been unable to reach the army to convey information on this matter."

Ilya nodded readily, he had at least figured out this last part.

"Dismayed as I was to encounter the Queen and the young King, the Queen had not yet been recognized, and so I was able to use my rank to shelter her for a time by preventing the examination of her affects. The King had not yet been discovered, and as you well know, I kept him hidden in my room."

Alexei tugged on his sleeve, and Anatoliy stopped.

"I wanted to tell you," said Alexei. "But Mama said not to tell you anything because it would put you in more danger."

"I see." Ilya flushed, rubbing the back of his neck absently. To think that he'd been hired to transport the young King without knowing; and that he had treated him so dismissively as well. He looked down at the tile.

"After a while," said Anatoliy, "I was no longer able to have the Queen visit my rooms because the rumors were becoming too pervasive and risked both of our covers. I do sincerely apologize, your Majesty."

Alexei sighed and squeezed his eyes shut. "I know. I don't

hold it a—" Ilya could tell he was about to start crying. The boy sniffled and wiped his eyes, then began to explain again. "I couldn't get to Mama to ask her if it was okay, but I knew she was in trouble and I had to do it myself. I decided to be brave like you said. I sent the doves anyway. I told them where we were. I knew they couldn't show up in time to save me or Mama, but it was the only way to keep you from getting killed." He trailed off, and Anatoliy took up.

"The young king also doubtless knew that the army was in position to retake Stosla and could not continue waiting. They needed the signal regardless of His Majesty's personal arrival. However, the handwritten note was an idea of his own.

"When General Boris arrived at Castle Tyrna, he of course immediately required the handover of the Queen's personal effects. I knew what would result from this but could do nothing, as the Queen had been separated from me for some time. The box contained many documents and items with the royal seal specifically designed to prove her identity. However, the fact that her son was traveling with her was not immediately evident.

"I had suspected that Alexei was getting out from time to time, though he had hidden his disappearances from me. When I returned to my rooms that day, I found that he was gone. Instead, I found a note. He had warned me that he was about to reveal himself. I had little time. I slipped into the passage in the rock.

"This was a room I had requested by design, so that it would be easier for me to move about as a spy and escape if necessary. The crown well knows about the secret passages at Tyrna, and we know them better than the Vroek Coalition— the castle was ours before it was theirs, after all.

"I slipped back to the dungeon to release Alexei. His Majesty had been there for only a few minutes."

Ilya breathed a sigh of relief.

"Then we went to the tunnels, which was something I'd been reluctant to try earlier, but His Majesty had left me with no choice. There was a lengthy, hidden path which I was aware of, but had never traveled before. We walked for miles in the dark under the earth until we came up in the neighboring region. It took several days for us to reunite with the army, and finally, to reach the Capitol."

"I knew nothing of this!" exclaimed Ilya, trying to contain his emotion but failing. The faces of Alexei and the others, along with the bright banners and flowers swam around him. "Everything that I thought was real… why, I didn't know, but I thought… I thought you had been killed. I thought that they were going to kill you." He clasped the boy's hand.

"They were," said Anatoliy grimly. "That part was real. Trust me that Boris no longer lives. He died by my hand."

This time Ilya wept openly and honestly. "But I don't understand. It is not just that you are a child, but especially knowing that you are the King… why, surely you have duties, obligations, you are needed, and so what is a smuggler and a deserter? I am nothing."

Alexei spoke. "Don't you remember what you said? A king has to protect his subjects. If he's a good king, anyway."

"But what about my crimes?" his voice shook.

Alexei smiled. "Do you think I would bring you here and not pardon you for past offenses? We shall be friends forever, I think."

Ilya looked up at him.

"Now, you don't have to keep sitting on the floor. Please, stand up."

Ilya slowly stood up from the floor. "Thank you. Your Majesty, Aleksandr, sir."

The boy laughed. "Call me Alexei."

The new courtiers, much moved by the sight they had just seen, broke into a light applause. After the two of them had departed from the hall, they spread this tale far and wide throughout the land, and that is how it has come to you, my dear reader.

The End.

The Strange People

By Maria Fedina

Chapter 1

S arah Smith stood in the doorway, hating everything.

After a particularly tiresome week at work, she'd been looking forward to a nice, relaxing night to kick off the long weekend, but one look at the kitchen told her that wasn't going to happen.

Pots and pans and breakfast dishes were still in the sink, empty pizza boxes and half-empty coffee cups on the table. Piles of half-folded laundry covered the sofa and chair in the living room. Not to mention dirty floors and an overflowing garbage bin.

She'd long made her peace with her cousins' more laid-back approach to housekeeping (Gwen at least *tried* to make an effort, most of the time, and Ella was always so busy that it was understandable, really), but she couldn't help thinking that it *was* inconsiderate of them to leave things in such a state, especially when they would be away all weekend on a special retreat.

Sarah did think it was strange; the middle of October seemed a bit late in the season for that sort of thing, and there was talk of bad weather approaching, but of course no one had asked *her*.

She began clearing the table, indulging in a number of muttered complaints to vent her irritation, though she stopped short before actual curses fell from her lips.

She wouldn't have liked it anyway, she told herself. Of that she was quite certain. She'd never been much for the outdoors, and lately even regular church services seemed to drain her. The relentless enthusiasm of some of the more exuberant members struck her as more off-putting than encouraging. Still, she could hardly help feeling somewhat neglected as she considered that they were now off with their friends on what would no doubt be a grand adventure filled with all manner of raptures and delights, while she was here, grumbling about having to clean up their mess.

There is no magic here.

The thought echoed in her mind as she took out the trash and washed the dishes, wiped down the counters and vacuumed the floors.

For a brief moment, she regarded her work with a degree of satisfaction, which was almost immediately snuffed out by the sense that there was *still* so much to be done. Here was an ever-growing collection of mismatched plastic containers and lids, there a drawer filled with every sort of cooking utensil imaginable except the particular one needed at any given moment, and everywhere, everywhere, far too many utterly useless decorative towels, which she half suspected came to life now and then to cannibalize what few good towels remained. She'd had more than one nightmare about being buried in large piles of *stuff*, and now seriously considered throwing it all out before there was any danger of such dreams coming true. But that was far too much work for one night.

She leaned pensively against the arm of the chair for some time before making up her mind that she *would* enjoy what was left of her night. Laundry could wait until tomorrow.

Thus rousing herself from her thoughts, she retrieved her work bag from where she'd left it and found the copy of *Phantastes* Grace had lent her.

She smiled at the thought of Grace. She liked the girl. Quick, efficient, not given to gossip—that alone made her an absolute gem of a coworker. It may have been a bit soon to consider her a *friend*, but they'd had some nice talks over the past few weeks, and she was sure that any book Grace recommended would be well worth reading. Besides, it *was* nice to be thought of.

She'd hardly opened the book when she realized there was something inside. It was a small envelope of shimmering sapphire, with her name carefully lettered in silvery script.

She took it out and looked it over, somewhat in awe of the simple elegance of it. Inside she found an invitation, reading:

You are cordially invited

to a time of prayer and fellowship

Saturday, 3–5pm

All weather.

Refreshments will be served.

She sat there for some time, turning the invitation over in her hands, wondering how, or even if, she ought to respond.

In small letters below that was the name of a church she'd never heard of before, and an address in a part of town she rarely visited. She felt some trepidation at the thought of venturing out into unknown territory. She always *tried* to keep an open mind, but she'd endured more than a few events where the preaching was lackluster at best, and the promised fellowship proved to be sorely wanting. Those disappointments had made her somewhat wary.

But then, it had been some time since she'd been personally invited to anything, and besides, she trusted Grace. She hesitated—hoped—prayed for… she didn't know what, and at last texted her a simple *thanks*.

Late as it was, she half expected Grace to be asleep already, so it came as a surprise when her phone buzzed with an almost instant reply.

So you'll come?

Another moment's hesitation, and then—

I'll be there.

It *was* nice to be thought of.

That night she dreamed of trees and mountains rising up around her until they towered overhead, and clouds and thick darkness which fell heavily upon everything until she was sure she must have been buried, and a small wooden door that appeared out of nowhere, outlined in a strange light. It glowed softly at first, then grew brighter and brighter until everything was impossibly white.

She ducked behind a thicket as she heard someone approaching from the other side and instinctively covered her eyes as the knob turned. The next moment, she felt, rather than heard, an explosion, and when she opened her eyes again, the door was gone, the light had faded, and she was, by all appearances, alone again, on the edge of a small clearing, just as it was beginning to snow. For some time she waited in darkness and silence, until at last she looked up and realized the sky was full of stars.

Eventually, the silence was broken by a rustling near the center of the clearing, and then the sound of a horn ringing out, the echoes of which soon mingled with the sound of other horns and flutes and voices answering in harmony from all quarters.

The mountains lit up with pinpricks of light as houses now appeared with candles in the windows, and the invited guests drew near bearing torches and lamps. The stars also grew brighter and came down with the snow until they rested on the treetops and among the branches, waking all the birds and forest creatures and illuminating the multitude that now descended upon the clearing, which seemed to grow to accommodate them all.

Now came men and women, elders and children, riding in on horses, in carriages, and on sleds, all dressed in their finest apparel, in white and gold, blue and silver, rich reds and dark greens. Greetings and gifts were exchanged, fires were lit, and baskets and trays of food and drink were laid upon a richly set table that now appeared beneath the tallest tree. Some brought out instruments and began to play, while others danced or walked about, and still others gathered here and there to talk or play games.

Sarah quite forgot herself as she silently watched the scene unfold from her place in the thicket. She took particular interest in the group nearest her, which consisted of a number of couples who had tired of dancing and now sat down around a small fire, talking and laughing together. Their clothes were dazzling—exquisitely embroidered silk and velvet, trimmed with glittering jewels and pearls and tinkling bells. But more striking than their attire was the kindness and candor in their expressions, and the unmistakable grace and courtesy of their manners.

Though their words were lost to the wind, it was clear that their wit was well matched and well aimed, and their mirth never came at another's expense. They were undoubtedly the best sort of people, and the longer Sarah watched, the more she wished she could join them.

As if hearing her thoughts, one of the young men now looked back and met her gaze. He seemed surprised only for a moment before rising and waving at her to come and sit by the fire. She gasped and stepped back, instantly aware of how out of place she was there. Her hair was windblown, her hands rough and cracked, her clothes and shoes worn and torn and paint-stained, and her manners hardly equal to such fair company. Still he beckoned her to come, and now the others were looking as well.

Some looked as shy of her as she was of them, but they rose to greet her all the same. Seeing she still hesitated, one of the gentlemen drew near with a smile so warm and welcoming that Sarah could hardly refuse to take the hand he offered. With his other hand, he reached down into the thicket and drew out a fine white cloak, and the next moment, Sarah found herself enveloped in warmth as it hung snugly around her shoulders.

Now when they had sat down once more, one of the ladies brushed and braided her hair, while another offered her a pair of fine red boots, and they all poured drinks and passed around plates of food before resuming their previous conversation.

Sarah listened in wonder as they spoke of all sorts of things, until at last the first rays of morning appeared in the east, and the merry scene faded from view.

Chapter 2

"What do you want?"

"I don't know."

"Well, that's not good."

Sarah sighed and reminded herself that she *did* like Grace, even if she had woken her up at a preposterous hour to pepper her with questions.

What's in your bag? Your pantry? Your library?

What would you do with a million dollars?

You have twenty-four hours' notice that you must leave your home. What do you take?

Those had been simple enough to answer, as she'd always liked being prepared and had a fairly active imagination. But now she felt they were getting into the tricky questions.

"Is all this really necessary?" Sarah asked.

"It *is*," Grace insisted. "You'll understand later. Now, come on, think. *What do you want?*"

Sarah sighed again.

Funnily enough, the night before, she *had* wanted to get up early. Gwen and Ella always extolled rising early as one of the highest virtues—easy for *them* to say when they didn't have to work nights—but she supposed they did have a point. If she couldn't do anything *exciting* or *important*, she could at least try to be *productive*. But morning had come too soon, and the house was cold, and her bed was warm, and her dreams had been so pleasant, that she'd wanted nothing more than to sleep as long as possible and dream on and on.

She knew, of course, that would be a very dull answer, but then, she supposed she herself was a terribly dull person. She considered saying as much to Grace, but thought better of it.

"All right," Grace said at last, "you don't have to tell me, if you'd rather not. But do think about it, and try to write *something* down."

Sarah promised she would, and upon hanging up, thought so deeply for so long that she might have fallen back asleep if not for the sudden appearance of the neighbors' cat in her window, pawing at the screen and begging for attention.

She grumbled at it affectionately before rising to open the window, only for it to leap off the sill and dart away. She sighed once more, refilled the water bowl hidden in the flower box, and supposed she had better get on with her day.

When she finally emerged from her room, she found that the piles of laundry had grown overnight, along with all the other piles of stuff. She wondered, not for the first time, whoever needed so much stuff? Certainly not her.

But of course, most of it belonged to her cousins. After all, it *was* their house, really, and it *was* very kind of her aunt and uncle to let her live there as well, and she *was* grateful to them all, and if her room was the smallest and her share of rent the biggest and she never *really* felt quite at home there, well, she could hardly complain about that, could she?

She *did* want to complain. Bitterly. But she contented herself with a cup of coffee and a prayer.

Behold, how good and how pleasant it is for brethren to dwell together in unity…

Her mood did pick up a little as she moved the clothes, none too neatly, onto her cousins' beds, and now she dove into cleaning up and clearing out with something like reckless abandon.

She began in her own room, emptying out her closet and drawers, keeping only the things she actually liked, and unsentimentally consigning the rest to the trash. She moved on to the kitchen, where she threw out anything that was undoubtedly expired, and uttered another prayer, this time of thanks that no one had been poisoned. Sarah filled an entire garbage bag with moldy fruit and rotten vegetables, week-old leftovers and crusty year-old condiments, and, most alarmingly, nearly everything in the medicine cabinet. Finally, she packed up the extra dishes, towels, and anything that wasn't being used into boxes which she left conspicuously on the table for her cousins to look through at their leisure, with a note suggesting they might be more appreciated elsewhere.

At last, she looked upon the results like an artist considering a fresh canvas, full of potential and possibility. It did look a bit empty; no doubt her cousins would have something to say about that when they returned, but then they could hardly complain about her tidying up a bit, could they?

The thought left her somewhat deflated, but the next moment she set it aside and resolved that she *would* enjoy her weekend.

As the time to leave drew near, she put a little more effort than usual into her appearance and tried to calm her nerves. She left early and was somewhat relieved to find the address easily enough, though she had to look twice to make sure she'd gotten it right.

The building was one she'd never seen before, and probably wouldn't have noticed even now if it hadn't been for the small hand-painted sign by the road, which was little more than a large shed, some distance from the road and partly hidden by a line of trees. Next to it was a small parking lot where half a dozen cars already sat. As she pulled in, she found that there were in fact two buildings, as the church itself sat in a state of construction a little further back, and the smaller building served as the fellowship hall.

Her first glimpses of the room revealed little, but it looked very plain. As soon as she had crossed the threshold, however, she felt as though she had stepped into an old holiday catalog she remembered from when she was a child, as elegance and simplicity met in a charming display. It seemed Christmas had come early here. Fragrant potted firs stood on either side of the door, decked with red and gold ribbons and glittering paper snowflakes, and the walls were hung with garlands.

At one end of the room was a beautifully set table laden with all sorts of refreshments. There were coffee and tea and cider served in teacups, fresh fruit and homemade doughnuts, meat and cheese, veggies and dip. At the other end, there was a small platform and a number of benches.

Grace was by her side at once. The girl greeted her with a warm smile and a hot cup of tea before quickly introducing her all around. Here were young Mr. and Mrs. Taylor, expecting their first child, and old Mr. and Mrs. Lewis, sharing photos of their grandchildren. Here was Pastor Tom Harper, neither young nor old, lately come from the east with his wife and six children, who now gathered around Sarah and asked ever so politely what she had in her pockets. They watched with the greatest delight as she pulled out a tiny pocketknife, a fountain pen, a compass, a comb, a ribbon, her wallet and keys, and a tissue.

Then there was also Mr. Hall, a widower with two young children; his sister Ellen; and his friend Mr. John Andrews. They greeted her with a degree of formality that was a little strange, but comforting in a way. It was as though everyone understood there was a way things ought to be done, but for once, the rules didn't seem like a mystery to her.

Once everyone had arrived, they soon settled in, and the pastor commenced the study. His prayer was refreshingly simple and to the point, with all reverence, no theatrics, and no wasted words. He read a few passages of Scripture without comment before adding a few words of his own.

"At the risk of sounding alarmist," he began, "I believe our first order of business is to come to terms with the fact that we are, in fact, at war."

At this, the small boys who had been fidgeting in the front row sat up a little straighter.

"We have been from the beginning," he continued, "but it is more evident at some times than others. We will not endanger those we love by running headlong into the fray, but neither will we run and hide when the battle comes upon us, nor will we be so foolish as to think that once upon a time, the devil prowled about as a roaring lion and disguised himself as an angel of light, but these days there's no need for caution. God help us, for we are often forgetful and blind to the dangers before us."

He prayed again, and now his litany was a little irregular as he prayed against rats and bats and shadows in the hall, cancer and chemicals and bad laws written by fools and tyrants, but the people took no notice and answered *amen* all the same.

"And now," he said, "on to the fellowship."

With that, the children ran outside to play, while the men rose from their places to move the table closer to the center of the room, and the ladies helped rearrange the benches. This being done, Mr. Hall hung a large, hand-drawn map on the wall before taking a seat at the head of the table.

"Before we begin," he said, "does anyone have anything to share?"

Mr. Lewis now stood and gave a small bow before beginning with great solemnity, "I wish to report a most honorable feat of great skill and patience, the disentangling of a most perplexing web."

Beside him, his wife laughed lightly before speaking to her neighbor in a mock whisper, "I untangled a necklace."

"My late mother's necklace," he continued, not the least bit deterred from his praises, "which I'd hoped to pass on to our eldest granddaughter. It was as delicate as a spider's web and I found it at the bottom of the jewelry box all knotted up tight as a string. I took one look at it and quite gave up hope, but she managed it somehow, and now look!"

He held up the necklace in question for all to see.

"Excellent!" Mr. Hall laughed and clapped his hands, and the rest of the table followed suit. "Who else?"

Now it seemed nearly everyone had some story to tell and some honor to bestow upon another, as they recounted wise words and charitable deeds done in secret over the course of the past week, which they now brought to light for the general admiration of the group. No accomplishment was deemed too small for their notice, but each one was celebrated as a great triumph worthy of praise.

At last their attention turned to Sarah, and she felt herself growing red as her mind went thoroughly blank. The others must have noticed her discomfort, because they all smiled encouragingly at her, and after a moment, Ellen asked in a pleasant, conversational tone, "So, did you do anything in particular this week?"

"Nothing important," Sarah answered, trying to keep her tone light. "I just…cleaned my house and went to work."

To her surprise, another cheer went up all around, and Mr. Hall immediately produced a tin of cookies, which they began passing around the table.

"Fantastic!" he cried with perfect sincerity. "See, you've got the hang of it already!"

The others laughed at her confusion, but so pleasantly that she couldn't help joining them.

"Now you'll have to tell her the story," Ellen said.

"Alright," he said. "Well, you see, a few years back I worked for a real ogre of a man. Always grumbling about something or other, never pleased with anything. Every day he'd come in and ask what I'd done, and every day I told him, *This and that, just like you said,* and he'd just look at me a minute and then say, *What, do you want a cookie for that?* like he was looking to start a fight. Now, I wasn't expecting a parade or anything for just doing my job, but I got to thinking, there was no need for him to be so *miserable* about it. So one day he asked me, *Do you want a cookie for that?* And I said, *You know, I think I would.* And I pulled out a box and started eating one right there. Of course I offered him one as well, and he didn't really know what to say after that. That is, until the next day, when he asked if I wanted a sticker." Here he picked up another, smaller tin and shook it with a grin. "I asked if he wanted a racecar or a rocket ship."

"Suppose he'd asked if you wanted a parade?" Mr. Andrews said.

"I was hoping he would, but I guess he learned his lesson."

"It *is* nice to appreciate the little things, isn't it?" remarked Mrs. Lewis, once their laughter had died down.

"The key to a happy marriage and a happy life," Mr. Lewis agreed, elbowing Mr. Taylor lightly.

Now they went on to the real game, in which everyone took turns telling a story. At least, it did *seem* like only a game, as Mr. Taylor asked Pastor Harper, *What news of the great dragon?* and Mrs. Taylor questioned Miss Mary Harper about the price of her wares, but Sarah had second thoughts when the girl took out a baby blanket and declared three dozen eggs would be payment enough, and Ellen offered Grace a bracelet for a box of candles. From time to time, challenges were given and dice were rolled, though Sarah suspected they didn't really matter in the end, as everything always seemed to work out one way or another.

At first she only watched and listened, but after a while, the others began asking her questions. The first came from Ellen.

"You're asked to investigate a house that's reported to be haunted. How do you proceed?"

"Check for a gas leak?" Sarah said, then met Ellen's gaze with an apologetic smile, worried she'd be annoyed that she wasn't taking the game seriously. On the contrary, Ellen looked delighted.

"Excellent! Then what?"

"Carbon monoxide? Black mold? Lead poisoning?"

"Anything else?"

"Is the homeowner available for questioning?"

"He is. And he is *not* crazy."

"Of course not. Well, does he have any idea why this might be happening? Been under any stress lately? Any great sin weighing on his conscience? Dabbling in the occult?"

"Hmmm. No…"

"Is he *sure* about that?"

Ellen thought a moment before saying with the utmost seriousness, "He's sure there's something trying to get into his house."

"Alright. I suggest he reinforce his doors and windows, ask the neighbors to keep an eye out, take a vacation, and speak to a pastor as soon as possible."

Ellen smiled and nodded approvingly, then passed her a plastic knife without explanation. As the game went on, she soon traded it for a butter knife, and then a cheap pocket knife, and at last a very nice silver letter opener, which she could easily imagine to be a gleaming sword. She also found herself in possession of a box of matches, an assortment of candles, a pocket hymnal, and a number of stickers from Mr. Hall's collection.

It was, altogether, such a cheerful and pleasant gathering that she was sorry when the time came for it to end, expecting to find that the house which just a few hours ago seemed so full of potential would now feel sadly empty in comparison.

As people began to leave, she lingered a while by the door, admiring the trees, when Grace came up behind her.

"Well? How did you like it?"

"It was wonderful."

"So we'll see you again next week?"

Her smile brightened as Sarah nodded.

"I do have one question."

"Oh?"

"Do the dice rolls actually mean anything?"

Grace laughed. "Not really, but here's something real."

She gestured to the tree. "Every snowflake has a name and a need. You don't have to take one if you don't want to—"

"No," Sarah said quickly. "I want to help."

Grace smiled broadly.

"Alright," she said, "how about this one?"

The note on the back read, *Joy Thompson, Maple Street, help with firewood.*

Sarah knew Miss Thompson to be about seventy years of age, that she lived alone with an undetermined number of cats, and had something of a reputation for chasing neighborhood youths from her yard. Of course, the neighborhood youths had a reputation of their own for causing mischief, so she could hardly blame the old woman for not welcoming their presence.

She accepted the snowflake and, in the spirit of the evening, thanked Grace for her assistance in setting her upon a most noble quest.

In short time, her quest brought her to an old Victorian style house on a quiet street. She parked some distance away and looked to see if anyone was home.

A figure, tall and thin, suddenly appeared on the porch, took a few shuffling steps forward, and then just as suddenly disappeared from view. Sarah stopped and stared for a moment, then ran as she realized what had happened.

She found the old woman lying on the ground, a little shaken but not seriously injured. She rose slowly, even with help, and dusted herself off without a word before turning her attention to her guest.

"Well. Thank you, Miss…"

"Sarah Smith, from down the street."

"I see." She looked her up and down before asking pointedly, "Can I help you with something?"

"I was just wondering if you might like some help with your firewood."

Miss Thompson looked at her doubtfully a moment before saying, "I can't afford to pay you."

"That won't be necessary," Sarah replied quickly.

"It's a big job."

"I have time."

Miss Thompson considered her a moment longer, then nodded, evidently satisfied, before pointing her to the woodpile and the basement door. She was undoubtedly very particular in her instructions, but Sarah found this was not without reason, as the basement was poorly lit, the steps somewhat slippery, and the wood liable to fall if not stacked properly. She made one trip, then another, and another. It wasn't too hard, but did get somewhat tedious, and she couldn't help feeling discouraged after she'd made at least thirty trips and the pile still had hardly a dent in it. After about an hour had passed, however, Miss Thompson came down herself.

"That'll be enough for tonight."

"I'll come back and finish it later," Sarah offered.

There was a pause, and then, "You don't have to do that."

"I'd like to," Sarah said with a smile.

Miss Thompson smiled back. "Well. You must be tired. Why don't you come in and have some tea before you go."

Sarah was shown upstairs to the kitchen, which seemed to be a perfect time capsule. The furniture was made of wood, very plain but solidly built, and the curtains and tablecloths were a simple white lace. Copper pots and cast-iron pans hung from the walls, and a large display case held an assortment of fine china plates, teacups, and saucers, crystal bowls, and a silver tea set.

"You like that, do you?" said Miss Thompson, coming in behind her.

Sarah nodded. "It's very nice."

"That's quality stuff, is what that is," she said. "I've never been rich, but I never get anything but the best if I can help it. You'd do well to remember that."

"Some people would say it's wasteful," Sarah ventured to remark.

"Some people are fools," came the quick reply. "The trouble with people these days is they just don't know the *value* of things. They'll toss precious family heirlooms to the curb without a thought because it doesn't fit with their decor, then fill their houses with worthless junk that breaks the minute you look at it funny and think they're saving money because they got it on sale, then try to offload their trash on others and call it charity. And then they call it a waste to buy nice things and keep them nice.

That Daniels woman down the street, she's very *nice*, isn't she? Last week she comes by with her nose in the air and says, *Who are you saving all that for, hmm?* I tell her I'm not saving anything. It's all in use, and who I leave it to when I'm gone is hardly any of her concern. Then she starts fussing at me because of the flowers. Ha! Did you hear about that?"

Sarah shook her head.

"I expected everyone would, the way she was carrying on about it. Do you know, her daughter came into my garden last month when she thought I wasn't home. Now, I wouldn't begrudge the child a flower or even a bouquet if she'd asked, but she went and picked *every last one* of my roses. Not a single one was left. Then her mother had the audacity to complain because I shouted at her poor little darling, as though a child of ten couldn't possibly be expected to know any better."

Now they sat down and Miss Thompson poured some tea. Her manners might not have been particularly genteel, but she proved to be a most gracious hostess all the same, and Sarah in turn did her best to be a gracious guest, and talked with a good deal of enthusiasm about her job and her home and her cousins and the retreat.

"Oh? And what are they doing there?" Miss Thompson now asked.

Sarah shrugged. "Camping, hiking, probably a good deal of

singing, and I expect they'll have a few interesting speakers."

"Do you think it will do them any good?" Miss Thompson asked seriously.

Sarah shrugged again. "I don't suppose it will do any harm."

"I hope not."

They sat in silence for a moment before the conversation turned to another topic. When at last it came time for them to part, they both declared that they had had a very pleasant visit, and should very much like to meet again sometime.

Upon returning home, Sarah imagined that some of the magic of the evening still lingered in the air, and now went to her cousins' rooms, folded their clothes, and put them away properly before settling down very comfortably with her book and reading late into the night.

That night, she dreamed again of the mountains, the very same, she was sure, that she'd seen the night before. But now the lights and music were behind her, and she found herself trudging through the snow after a line of people, climbing higher and higher. From the head of the line came a voice, hardly intelligible over the wind, shouting words of encouragement and urging the others onward and upward.

Sarah hurried to catch up to the people ahead, and found two girls, somewhat underdressed for the weather, but in remarkably good spirits, echoing the leader's words and talking excitedly about the journey ahead.

Soon they came to a comfortable looking house with candles in the windows. The inhabitants waved and called out for them to come in and rest a while, but they cheerfully answered that they could not stop, and to come along with them. Now a few of the young people did come out and join the line, and were met with much praise and applause from the travelers.

Sarah couldn't help noticing that unlike the first gathering, which had included people of all ages, most of her present companions seemed to be very young, and many of the newcomers seemed ill-prepared for the weather.

They soon came to another house. Here the inhabitants' greetings carried a tone of concern, as they urged the travelers to come in, rest, and warm themselves, wait out the storm and take provisions for their journey, but they answered resolutely that they could not stop for anything and walked on.

Now a few people hurried on ahead, while others began to grow tired and lag behind, but they all pressed on, heedless of the difficulty. Sarah found that she still wore the cloak and boots she'd been given the night before, and now her own clothes were also better suited for the weather, which gave her some advantage. Still, she knew that she was no longer exactly young, and as she watched the youths growing weary, she wondered how much longer she would be able to keep up.

They approached a third house. Its owner stood on the porch and waved urgently to the passersby, shouting to be heard over the wind which now blew heavily. As they drew near, whispers came down the line to be wary of such people, lest their resolve should break down with doubt and discouragement. Thus it happened that most of the travelers now thoroughly ignored the man as they passed, but a few grew angry and began to shout back, warning him to mind his own business and not criticize what he didn't understand.

Between the wind and the shouting, Sarah found it impossible to hear what he was saying, but as they passed the house, she caught sight of a large sign by the road, reading, *Danger: wolves ahead,* and in smaller letters below, *Blessed is the man who walks not in the counsel of the ungodly.*

There was a howl in the distance.

Now Sarah ventured to ask those nearest her where exactly they were going and for what purpose. They could give no satisfactory answers, but some simply ignored her, while others seemed shocked or annoyed that she didn't already know and said little more than *onward and upward.*

She pointed out the difficulty of the journey and wondered if there might at least be some better way.

"The leaders know," came the reply, and, "Sacrifices must be made," and then, "We're told to expect to suffer for doing good."

"Is this good?" she asked.

She received no answer, but the others pushed past her and went on ahead.

At last, they came to a sharp cliff. The voice, now only a distant echo ahead, continued urging them forward. Here some hesitated, while others went on heedless of the danger and disappeared into the darkness. A young man came up behind Sarah and tried to give her an encouraging smile.

"All things are possible for one who believes."

She thought a moment and answered quietly, "You shall not put the Lord your God to the test."

His expression hardened, and he turned away and walked on without another word. After a moment, she turned as well and began the long walk down the mountain, but paused to look back one last time, only to find the others already gone.

Sunday morning, she rose before her alarm, feeling so sore she wondered if she had jumped after all, until she remembered the events of the night before and how many armloads of firewood she had stacked. It had undoubtedly been a most productive day, and as she meant to keep it up, she wasted no time in getting up and getting ready.

If her cousins had been home, she might have had second thoughts about visiting another church, though she'd been wanting a change for some time.

She'd tried to explain once how discouraging it was to always hear that *good is the enemy of great*, and that settling for a simple, quiet life was a shameful waste of one's gifts and talents, and how all their bright promises for the future rang increasingly hollow with each passing year, but they had only looked at her with a mix of annoyance and pity and said she was just overthinking things as usual.

She texted Grace to ask if she was going, and readily accepted her offer to ride together. They arrived early and found the parking lot already considerably more full than it had been the night before. Once they had gone inside and settled in, she found herself seated between Grace and Mr. Andrews. As they waited to begin, she couldn't help noticing him glancing over. He blushed slightly as he caught her gaze, but said nothing as the service now began.

The hymn selection was excellent. They sang *I bind unto myself today the strong name of the Trinity*, and *I walk in danger all the way*, and *A mighty fortress is our God* with far more strength and feeling than Sarah was used to hearing on Sunday mornings, as Mr. Lewis played skillfully on the accordion. Then the pastor read from the book of Colossians, spoke on the need to be charitable without being naïve, that they might not be cheated of their reward, and prayed against thieves and robbers and deceivers of all sorts.

When it was over, the building quickly emptied as people went outside to continue talking, and Sarah found herself standing by the door with Mr. Andrews, who offered her an apologetic smile.

"I'm sorry," he said, "I didn't mean to stare. I was just thinking, that's a beautiful Bible."

It *was* beautiful, with its gilt pages, gold ribbon, and real leather cover, but she couldn't help blushing and frowning slightly.

"It was a gift," she said a little curtly, "from my godmother. I *do* read it."

"I didn't doubt that," he said mildly.

Her blush deepened. "I'm sorry. I just thought—"

"What?"

"It's nothing—it's stupid—it's just, well, you know what they say about Bibles that are falling apart."

"Ah. Yes," he said thoughtfully, "that *is* a point of pride for some people, and yours looks practically new. Your godmother was wise to give you something that wouldn't fall apart after a few years."

"She was," Sarah agreed warmly.

Her parents may not have been particularly devout, but they'd liked the sound of their child having a godmother, and to her credit, the friend they had chosen had taken her role very seriously and considered it her utmost duty to instruct her goddaughter in the fundamentals of religion. The truly extravagant gifts had been few and far between, and though they had sometimes embarrassed Sarah a little, she couldn't deny that they were very nice, and exceedingly practical.

Here their conversation was momentarily interrupted as a number of young girls ran up to them.

"We're going to have a ball!" they cried gleefully, jumping up and down and clapping their hands before running off to tell another group. Ellen trailed after them, smiling.

"I suppose you've heard the news," she said. "Some of the girls are planning a Christmas ball."

"Are they?" said Mr. Andrews. "I do hope we're invited."

"Do you?"

"Of course. I can't say I'm much of a dancer, but I guess there are worse ways to spend an evening."

"Are you going to ask her?" Sarah asked once Ellen had left.

"No."

The quickness of his answer and the confusion in his tone surprised her, and she couldn't help asking, "Why not?"

"She's Jack's sister," he said, as though that explained everything. He glanced over to where Mr. Hall now stood with his children. "You know, she's lived with them ever since his wife died. I don't know how he ever would have managed without her. It'd be one thing if she was unhappy. If he was an ogre and a tyrant, and she was a damsel in distress, I guess I could play at being a knight in shining armor. But they've got a good thing going, and I'd hate to break that up. Still, it *is* the sort of thing that makes you wish…"

He looked a little wistful, sighed and shook his head, then smiled and bid her good afternoon.

For some time she stood there, lost in thought, but at last she came to herself once more, and looking around, soon found a familiar face in a tall, somewhat awkward young man. She recognized him at once as Henry Morton, an admirer of her cousin. He was, perhaps, a tad too excitable to suit her, but a good, steady,

Christian man all the same, and she was sure she hadn't imagined the looks that had sometimes passed between him and Gwen. Last spring, she had fully expected to hear news of some sort of announcement, but none had come, and then after a while, she hadn't seen very much of him anymore. As she wondered about this, he recognized her as well, and immediately came over to greet her.

"How's Gwen?" he asked, after the initial pleasantries had been exchanged. "Have you heard from her lately?"

"Not…very recently. You know she and Ella went on a retreat with some friends from church."

"Yes," he said slowly. "I did hear something about that."

He looked as though he were going to say something more, then reconsidered. There was a long pause, and at last he leaned in a little closer and asked in a low voice, "How is she, really?"

Sarah's first instinct was to answer *fine,* but there was something in his tone and manner that gave her pause, and it occurred to her that Gwen *had* seemed a little busier than usual in the past few weeks, a little tired, and more than usually flustered.

"I don't know," she said at last. And then, seeing the utter dejection on his face—"But I'll let you know."

She gave him what she hoped was an encouraging smile,

which he returned with a look of deep gratitude before wishing her a good afternoon.

She found Grace deep in conversation with Ellen, and not wanting to interrupt, turned her attention to the snowflakes hanging from the trees. Many of the needs were simple—*a cheap sewing machine, groceries, boys' shoes, size 7 ½*—while others were more involved—*help with errands, a ride to the airport*. She took a few and slipped them into her Bible.

One that particularly intrigued her said only *Julia Gray—peace and quiet*. She was just looking it over when Grace and Ellen approached, and she now learned that this was in fact the topic of their conversation.

Julia was a friend of Ellen's and an aspiring writer whose chief complaint was that she never had the time or space or energy to write. From Ellen's expression, it was clear that there was more to the story, but she didn't elaborate, and Sarah thought it best not to press. They had been strategizing about the best way to help her and settled on coming over the next day to cook and clean and do whatever else needed to be done, before helping her set up a nice little workspace where she could write in peace, with no distractions or excuses. Upon learning that Sarah would be free, Ellen now invited her to join them, an invitation which Sarah happily accepted.

Sometime later, she returned to Miss Thompson's and found

her in her garden, trimming back some blackberry bushes.

"I don't need any more wood today," she said, "but if you have a few minutes, I could use some help with my computer. I don't know what happened, but suddenly everything on the screen is too big."

Sarah obliged and quickly found the problem, and then accepted Miss Thompson's invitation to stay for tea. She told her about her morning and the church, about Grace and Ellen and Mr. Andrews and the ball, and also about Henry Morton, and some of her own concerns that had been growing since their conversation. Miss Thompson looked thoughtful.

"Did she give any particular reason for breaking things off with him?" she asked after a minute.

Sarah shrugged. "I suppose she was just…too busy."

"Busy with *what*, exactly?"

No doubt it was something important, but Sarah admitted she couldn't for the life of her remember. Miss Thompson clucked her tongue and shook her head.

"Well," she said at last, "I can't say whether this Morton fellow is your cousin's Prince Charming or knight in shining armor or what have you, and for all I know she might have had a very good reason for refusing him, not that she needs one. But I do hope she knows what she's about.

"Believe it or not, I was young once," she continued, "and heard all about how the world was ending, and all the talk about a fresh new generation rising up and taking the world by storm just before the last trumpet sounds. And I've seen far too many young people ready to sacrifice themselves, with all their hopes and dreams and plans for the future they don't expect to come, and get so caught up expecting to die, that they never stop to consider what will happen if they *live*. And then the years pass and things don't quite pan out the way they expected, and one day they realize they no longer have all of the options and opportunities they once did, and of course they make the best of it, but in the end, they can't help feeling a bit cheated."

That night, Sarah dreamed again of the mountains, bright and sparkling as the full moon fell upon the new fallen snow, but the beauty was somewhat spoiled by a dark circle in the earth. As she approached, the wind blew colder and the shadows seemed to grow sharper, even as the swirling snow momentarily obscured her view of everything else. Still she pressed on, and at last found that some of the shadows were people, gathered as though around a fire, their forms blanketed by a strange sort of mist, and there was one among them, darker than the rest, whom she perceived to be speaking.

The speaker's voice was muffled by wind and mist, but its meaning was clear enough. It spoke great, swelling words, one moment praising its listeners' strength for coming so far, and the next berating them for their weakness. It struck Sarah that if she could see and hear as the others did, she might have thought it impressive, inspiring, even attractive, but as it was, something was terribly wrong.

She suddenly felt terribly exposed and prayed that it might not see her. She felt a thrill of terror run through her as she imagined its eyes now fixed upon her, and the next moment breathed a sigh of relief as she felt a barrier had suddenly arisen between them, shielding her from its view.

As she looked about the circle, she found there was one among the listeners who was less shrouded than the rest, a young woman now crying from cold and exhaustion. The others around her clearly told her to hush, utterly enraptured by the speaker's words, but her misery was too great to be concealed any longer. Whether Sarah's shield now extended to the girl as she drew near and knelt beside her, or the others just doubled their efforts to ignore her, Sarah was not sure, but she felt quite certain they would not be noticed. She looked carefully at the girl's face and tried to touch her arm, only to find that the girl was completely intangible. The mist was not. Sarah recoiled as she felt the sensation of touching a spider's web, then brushed her fingers against the snow before returning to her work.

As she did so, she tried to whisper some words of encouragement in the girl's ear, only to find that words now utterly failed her. She thought a moment longer and took courage as she remembered the words of that morning's hymns. She began to sing, softly at first, then louder and louder until her voice carried over the wind. Neither the girl nor the others seemed to hear, but by the time she was halfway through the first song, the girl seemed to have regained some of her strength and grown a little more solid than the shadows that held her, and now began working to clear away what remained of the mist.

At last she was completely freed. Sarah watched as her expression relaxed slightly and her breathing steadied, and she looked about her as if waking out of a trance.

The next moment, she began shaking violently as she once more became sensible of the cold.

Sarah quickly slipped off her cloak and put it around the girl's shoulders. She gasped, evidently feeling the change. Then, as she was still seated, Sarah proceeded to give her her boots as well. Perceiving that the speaker was still ignoring them, Sarah once again grabbed the girl's arm and found that while she still seemed unaware of her presence, she now rose and followed, and together they quickly slipped away from the circle and darted into the woods.

The way down the mountain proved to be more difficult than Sarah expected, as the further they went, the warmer it became. Soon the snow turned to slush, and there arose a fog so thick they could hardly see more than a few feet ahead. What was more, Sarah was sure that it *was* the same mountain she had traveled the previous night, but it was different now. There were no more cliffs, but neither were there houses. Where the last house should have been, there was only an empty clearing. Yet as they drew near, they found the sign, which now read, *Your Word is a lamp unto my feet and a light unto my path*, and beneath it was a lantern, burning so warm and bright that Sarah wondered that it didn't burn the girl when she picked it up. For a moment, they simply stood and stared in wonder, but soon the sky grew dark with clouds, the wind blew colder, and they heard the sound of wolves behind them. And so taking the lantern, they hurried on their way.

They soon came to where the next house should have been and found that it too had vanished. At first they could see nothing but shadows, but as their eyes adjusted, the light grew once more, and now they perceived a number of forms, hardly visible to the eye, moving about here and there. They seemed to be wrapped in a different sort of mist, which glowed softly with occasional flashes of color, like rainbows or auroras. One stopped before them, and when it passed, they found a pair of swords.

They had hardly gone far before there was a rumble of thunder overhead, and then a flash of lightning, and suddenly they were caught in a heavy downpour. They ran down the path, now slippery with mud, and heard on the wind what sounded like voices, some mocking their difficulties, others entreating them to be reasonable and turn back. Still they pressed on, and at last they came to a road, and then a house, real and solid, where they at once found a warm welcome, food and drink, hot baths, and warm beds. Until now, the girl had not acknowledged Sarah directly, but as they got ready for bed, their eyes met, and she smiled.

183

Chapter 4

Monday morning, Sarah, Grace, and Ellen arrived early at Julia Gray's house. They found her nervous and apologetic, and the house in a terrible state, with dirt and grime and garbage everywhere, and a strange sort of heaviness in the air. Ellen had explained that she lived with her sister and two or three of her sister's friends, who clearly had no qualms about taking advantage of others' hospitality. Though she'd tried her best, the resulting mess had quickly become too much for her to handle on her own.

They got to work at once and spent the morning filling bag after bag with trash, sorting mail and recyclables and loose change, washing windows and opening them wide to let the air in. They took brooms to the cobwebs lurking in dark corners, vacuumed and mopped, scrubbed and scoured, then did it all again for good measure. Anna Taylor dropped by with lunch, as well as a carpet cleaner, an air purifier, and new water filters. Sarah and Grace washed the dishes, organized the pantry, and made cookies and cakes, while Ellen brought in lamps and candles and hung Christmas lights to banish what remained of the darkness and gloom. Julia began to smile, then laugh, then almost cry with gratitude as she saw the transformation.

"A team of fairy godmothers couldn't have done it better," she exclaimed as they finally sat down in the living room to enjoy some coffee and cake.

"You'll remember that I *am* a godmother," said Ellen, "to my niece and nephew."

"As am I," said Grace. "So I guess this sort of thing is par for the course."

Sarah looked at them both, feeling only slightly surprised, before remarking, "Sadly, I'm neither a fairy, nor a godmother, but I'm happy to help all the same."

Grace and Ellen shared a look. Ellen shrugged and said, "Well, there's still time," and then, to Julia, "I *do* wish we could do more."

Julia sighed. "I don't suppose there's much anyone can do. Honestly, short of a miracle, I don't see things changing much. I'd hoped they would, when Jamie told me she'd made new friends at church, but *clearly*…"

She sighed again.

"*Are* they Christians?" Sarah asked.

"You know, I'm not sure," came the reply. "They might *say* so, and maybe they believe it. Now that I think of it, I'm not sure it *is* a Christian group, exactly, that they're part of. Anyway, I don't pretend to know their hearts, but I *can* say I haven't seen much evidence of it."

"Where are they now?" Sarah asked.

"Some retreat. They're supposed to be back tonight."

Now Sarah wondered if it might not be the same retreat as her cousins were attending, and Julia confirmed that it was, and asked what she knew about it.

"Not much," Sarah admitted ruefully. "The way they talk, you'd think they were doing something grand and glorious, or at least something *good*, but…"

She trailed off, and there was a long silence before Grace suggested they pray.

Sarah returned home late, half expecting to find Gwen and Ella already there, but the house was dark and the driveway empty. She made some tea and sat in the living room with her book to watch for them, but it was well past midnight before she saw their car coming down the driveway. She offered them fresh tea—which they declined—and waited for them to start talking about their adventure, or comment on the changes. To her surprise, they did neither, but waved off her questions about the retreat, evidently too exhausted for words. She began to talk a little about her weekend, but trailed off as she realized they weren't listening, and bid them goodnight soon after.

The next morning, however, they seemed to have recovered all their usual energy and then some. Sarah was surprised to find them still at home when she awoke, and still more surprised to find the house looking decidedly emptier than it had the night before. Not only had they cleared away the boxes on the table, but a number of other things as well. Knickknacks and books had been carelessly tossed into piles, along with a good deal of clothes.

Ella only rolled her eyes when she asked about it.

"Really, there are more important things in life than *money* and *stuff*."

Sarah didn't disagree, but couldn't help thinking it strange that they were throwing out some of their nicest things.

"You can have it, if you like," came the careless response.

Sarah asked, once or twice, if there was anything she could do to help, but this only seemed to irritate them, as though she should have known already without having to ask. At last they sighed and said it was *fine*, in a tone that clearly said it wasn't, and told her not to bother, so she didn't.

She tried once more to ask about their trip, but their answers were brief and revealed little, and they finally shook their heads and waved her off as if to say, *You wouldn't understand.* Efforts to interest them in her activities also failed, as they rolled their eyes and asked if she wasn't too old to be playing pretend. She found it terribly provoking, but there was little time to think about it now, as she *did* have to go to work, so at last she wished them a good afternoon and went her way.

She found the return to her usual routine easier than expected, as now even the most mundane tasks seemed to carry new meaning.

The enchantment of the evening lasted until she came home and found the lights still on and heard whispering coming from Ella's room, which fell silent the moment she knocked.

She didn't dream that night, or for several nights after that.

The Summons

A Salt and
Light Anthology

188

Chapter 5

The rest of the week saw a return to normalcy, broken up by a number of little quests. Tuesday, Sarah made a cake and a casserole for the neighbors three doors down, whose son was in the hospital. Wednesday, she helped the lady across the street with yard work. Thursday, she went shopping for children's shoes and winter clothes, which she dropped off at people's doorsteps after work, before taking the Lewis' neighbors to the airport for an early flight. Friday, she slept late.

It was late Friday night before she saw Gwen and Ella again, and she wondered at the change a week could make. She had come home a little earlier than usual and found them in the kitchen, tired and irritable. She couldn't help noticing they had hardly eaten all week, and she couldn't imagine they'd slept much either, as she'd heard them talking well past midnight nearly every night.

Now they were gathering ingredients and arguing over how many bowls they would need.

Sarah's first greeting was ignored, and her inquiry as to what they were doing was met with a sharp, "What does it look like?" from Gwen. She stared until Gwen looked away.

"Sorry," she mumbled. "I'm just…tired."

“Then sleep,” Sarah said. “We can’t.”

Sarah glanced over the recipes on the table and looked at the clock.

“I’ll be up late anyway. Just let me do it.”

“Fine!” Ella huffed before storming away.

“Are you sure?” Gwen asked doubtfully.

Sarah resisted the urge to roll her eyes as she started a pot of coffee. “I *am* capable of following a recipe.”

At last, Gwen relented, warned her to follow the recipes *exactly*, and went to bed. Sarah looked at the notecards and immediately saw there must have been some sort of trick, because all the recipes were wrong. She fixed them and spent the next few hours baking enough cakes, pies, tarts, and trifles for a small army.

She had slept only a few hours when she was awoken by the sound of voices. Opening her door a crack, she spied about a dozen people seated in the living room, listening with rapt attention to an energetic young man speaking with great passion and zeal on the absolute necessity of having a vision, a purpose, taking risks and embracing discomfort, and refusing to settle or waste their lives on dull, common, mediocre pursuits. He spoke also of the need to be spiritually minded, as good deeds and virtue alone couldn’t save anyone, nor Bible reading or church attendance or other acts of piety.

All this was true enough, and no doubt there were some that needed to hear it, for Sarah couldn't deny there were many good and decent people who were pagans through and through, and many theologians who turned out to be heretics and apostates. There were those who faithfully attended services all their lives, only to use their religion as a cloak of covetousness. Still, she wondered at his purpose for so easily casting aside the things that made for wisdom and discipline and good order. Were they of no value at all, and would good works done with bad motives be better left undone?

At last, she'd had enough of hiding. There was no chance of avoiding them entirely, but she opened her door as quietly as possible and tried to sneak past without drawing too much attention to herself.

The speaker came to an abrupt stop, confusion and annoyance flashing across his face before his expression smoothed into a look of serenity. The others also looked up as though a spell had been broken. She offered a polite smile and a nod, and the next moment it seemed a switch had been flipped, as the man greeted her with a too loud and too bright "Hello!" and the rest—Gwen and Ella included—were suddenly all smiles, clamoring for her to come and join them. She politely declined, stepping behind the kitchen counter to make a pot of coffee, but they persisted.

She couldn't deny that the man was quite charming, smiling as though he knew a great secret, which he was very eager to impart to his hearers. Likewise, the others seemed perfectly pleasant and agreeable, aside from their appalling lack of courtesy, as they'd left jackets and dishes and crumbs strewn everywhere, and some now sat with their shoes on the couch. They called themselves visionaries and kingdom builders, and began trumpeting their good deeds very loudly as they listed a number of charities they were fundraising for, none of which she'd heard of.

She smiled and apologized that she didn't have any money, but wished them the best in their efforts. She felt their dismissal, and a few moments later, they resumed their meeting. She quickly got her coffee and decided to leave early, taking the leftover desserts with her.

She found the driveway packed and her car completely blocked in. Undeterred, she grabbed her things and began walking. She arrived at the church a few hours later, and gratefully accepted Grace's offer of a ride home. She also saw Henry, and apologized that she didn't have any news. He smiled and thanked her anyway.

Julia came with Ellen and the children, and Sarah soon learned that she had just moved to a new place.

"I *am* sorry," she said, "for wasting all your time."

"Don't be ridiculous," Ellen said. "The rain falls on the just and the unjust, and we're told to do good to our enemies, so I'd hardly say it was a complete waste."

"She's not exactly my *enemy*."

"She's not exactly your friend, either," Sarah said.

Julia sighed deeply and shook her head. "I don't want to just give up on her, but…I *can't* help her, it wasn't getting better, and I just couldn't take it anymore."

Sarah smiled and commiserated, then changing the subject, asked if there was any more news of the upcoming ball. She learned a venue had been decided upon as well as a date, and a handful of invitations had already been printed.

She returned home late, found everyone gone, the house a disaster, and Gwen and Ella cleaning up, and presented them with the invitations. Ella hardly looked at hers before heading off to bed, but Gwen at least thanked her and said she would think about it.

Three weeks passed with little improvement, and Sarah felt the whole thing start to wear on her. After their initial flurry of activity, her cousins had fallen into a state of deep and perpetual irritation. She felt her mind growing fuzzy and her motivation to do much of anything slowly being sapped, as all her efforts were met with only indifference and scorn, and the gloom that seemed to cling to them now settled over the whole house. She thought she saw the lights flickering, heard scratching in the walls, and could have sworn she was being watched.

Now the little church became more and more of a sanctuary, and Sarah felt her spirit revive each week as they gathered with words of wisdom and encouragement, and used their gifts to build up one another. Her own talent for baking was much appreciated, and now she traded cakes and pies for candles and Christmas lights and other small treasures.

She dreamed again, but now all her dreams—they *were* only dreams, she told herself—were of a lurking darkness that threatened to consume all it touched. At first it only roamed the halls, then stalked outside her door, and then at last began knocking, pounding, demanding to be let in. She shut her eyes and hid under the covers. The noise continued. She shouted that it wasn't welcome and to go away. It made no difference. She prayed—the knocking faltered—and sang—she felt it step back.

She saw her advantage, and in a stroke of clarity, remembered her weapons. She sat up and fumbled about in the darkness a moment, and suddenly felt her hand wrap around the hilt of a sword. It glowed gently, and by its light she was able to light a lamp as well.

She awoke in the middle of the night, confused and short of breath and far more tired than she should have been, and oddly enough, clutching the silver letter opener that she'd kept in her drawer. She waited and listened and found that the deep darkness —*was* it real? —was gone, but now there was a knocking at the window. Her heart raced, but she sat up slowly and looked out, and found to her relief that it was only the cat. She fumbled for the latch and let it in, and as the night was unseasonably warm, decided to leave the window open so it could get back out on its own. The fresh air seemed to be just what she needed, and she soon drifted off comfortably to sleep.

The following morning, she sat in the living room with all the windows open, a cup of coffee in one hand and the letter opener in the other, watching as her uncle and one of his friends went through the house looking things over.

"That's definitely mold where the pipes are leaking," her uncle said, inspecting the cabinet under the kitchen sink. "There's mice or squirrels or something in the attic, that water heater should have been replaced years ago, and I'd like to have a word with the guy who installed that stove."

His friend raised an eyebrow and joked, "Have you ever

considered that your house might be cursed?"

"I'd say it was a blessing that we found out now," Sarah replied.

"True enough," he agreed. "Not to worry, we'll get this sorted soon enough."

She texted Gwen and Ella to let them know. Ella responded a few hours later to say they would be staying with friends for a few days.

That afternoon, she told Grace what had happened, accepted her offer to stay until the issues could be resolved, requested a week's vacation, and scheduled a meeting with Pastor Harper.

Chapter 7

Next came Thanksgiving. Sarah had been disappointed when her aunt and uncle called Sunday afternoon to say they would be out of town, and her cousins, unsurprisingly, had plans of their own.

She was just beginning to feel sorry for herself when she remembered Miss Thompson, and wondered if she had any plans. She did not, and as it turned out, neither did Grace or a number of others. Plans were quickly made, groceries bought, and the house prepared for company.

Thursday afternoon, her guests arrived with blessings and good wishes, and the afternoon was spent with plenty of good food and good cheer. She hoped Gwen and Ella were enjoying themselves half as much, wherever they were.

It wasn't until the next afternoon that she heard from Gwen.

I can't take it anymore, she wrote, then gave an address several hours west.

Now the adventure began. Sarah grabbed her keys and her bag, always ready, and coats and blankets, down and wool—it was cold and growing colder, and they'd hardly been prepared. She chased the sun and raced the moon, and could have sworn she heard the stars singing as she staved off sleep with a magical elixir of a large double espresso iced coffee. She drove through wind and fog and rain and sleet, and at last arrived, well past midnight, at a small parking lot near the base of a mountain. There were voices some distance away. She flashed her lights once, then twice, and thought about getting out and starting up the trail, when Gwen appeared, cold and weary, and ran to meet her.

"Where's Ella?" Sarah asked.

"Not coming. She wouldn't…wouldn't listen."

The voices drew nearer, and now the leader appeared, at first urging her to come back, then growing angry as he saw Sarah's car. The others stood and watched as he stepped into the road to block them in, and snarled and sputtered and tried to make himself intimidating. It almost worked, but as Sarah stared him down and turned her lights on, his bravado seemed to falter, and at last he nervously stepped back. They quickly went their way, Gwen shaking from cold and fear and breathing heavily.

"A girl went missing, you know," she whispered after a few minutes. "The last time. They said it was her own fault, she just wandered off. No one knows what happened to her."

They drove a little further before pulling into a gas station. Now Sarah thought she saw a familiar face in the girl just ahead of them. Their eyes met. Sarah smiled and waved. The girl waved back. Gwen looked as though she'd seen a ghost.

They drove on, and Sarah talked about work and church and
what they would wear to the ball—because of course Gwen *would*
come now—and Mr. Andrews and Mr. Morton and all sorts of
nonsense, until at last she saw that Gwen was asleep.

199

Sunday morning, Anna Taylor approached Sarah after church.

She smiled nervously and began, "Sam and I were wondering…if you might be willing…that is, if you would consider…being our child's godmother?"

She continued, "Neither of us have any family, and I'm afraid we don't know many people here, and, well, you did come highly recommended."

Her cousins didn't believe in godmothers, fairy or otherwise. No doubt they'd laugh or roll their eyes and think it was ridiculous. Maybe she wouldn't tell them.

She smiled and took Anna's hands in her own. "I would be honored."

The Summons

A Salt and
Light Anthology

200

The Hand-Knit Dog

By Laura Schiller

Chapter 1

"No dogs allowed in the building," said Jean. "I'm sorry."

"Not even a little one?" Norah asked quietly, cupping her hands in front of her to hold an imaginary ball of fur. "Something I could keep in my room? It wouldn't disturb the other tenants, I promise."

She knew it wouldn't do any good to ask, though. The man's face under his grey newsboy cap was regretful, but decided. He leaned on his mop, looked up from the patch of floor he was cleaning, and shook his head.

"Look, it's not up to me. The board voted on it, something about allergy risks. You could bring it up at the next tenant meeting if you like."

"Oh…okay. Maybe." Norah shrugged and looked down at her shoes. She was not the kind of woman who brought things up at meetings. Talking to strangers—or even acquaintances she didn't know well—made her break out in a cold sweat. Besides, she couldn't look someone who suffered from allergies in the face and let them think she didn't care.

"You could get a goldfish," Jean suggested hopefully. "Or a lizard. Anything that doesn't have fur or feathers. My son had a snake once that used to curl up on him like a cat. It was cute."

Norah shuddered internally at the thought of pop-eyed fish or scaly reptiles, but he was so clearly trying to cheer her up that she said, "I'll think about it. Have a nice evening."

"You too." The caretaker touched the brim of his newsboy cap, nodded, and went back to mopping.

Norah walked past him across the lobby. As usual, it was so tidy, she could hardly tell it needed cleaning. The linoleum gleamed. The cluster of armchairs stood at attention like soldiers, stiff and sleek in their navy blue upholstery. Even the smell was unwelcoming. The sharp sting of hand sanitizer had never gone away since the dispenser was first installed. She hated it, but sprayed her hands anyway before pressing the elevator button.

Her apartment was furnished in much the same style as the lobby, but at least it didn't smell like a hospital. It smelled like lemon and lavender; only cleaning fluids, but better than nothing. She had knitted blankets and embroidered tablecloths to throw over the stiff furniture, and filled vases with paper flowers that never wilted. Her last roommate had said it looked like an old lady lived here, but since that roommate had moved out two years ago, there was no one left to complain.

Norah was thirty years old, but she did feel like an old lady sometimes, except for all the times she felt like a child. The frantic noise and speed of modern life made her nervous. She worked from home, ordered her clothes online, and went to visit her parents on the other side of the country only for Christmas and New Year's. There were days when she didn't talk to another living soul except via text message. If she didn't force herself to take a walk every day after work, she would probably never leave her apartment.

Still, if only she didn't always have to walk alone…

She pulled up a classical music playlist on her laptop, curled up on her bed with a blanket around her shoulders, and opened the bag of yarn she had just bought at the Second Chance Shop. She'd always thought there was something poignant about second-hand yarn. What had it been once, before someone unraveled it? A child's blanket? An old woman's shawl? Did it still remember those it had once kept warm?

This ball of yarn was a creamy light brown, so soft she couldn't resist holding it to her cheek. She'd seen a dog with fur like that in the neighbourhood, walking with a spring in its step and wagging its tail. It had come up to Norah to sniff her hand.

Its owner had apologized profusely, misreading Norah's stillness as fear, but the dog had known better and had let her scratch its soft ears for several seconds before bounding away.

It had reminded her of something her mother used to say whenever they saw a dog with thick woolly fur. *"Ein Selbstgestrickter,"* she'd say, grinning. *"A hand-knit one."*

Norah glanced from the ball of yarn in her hand to her computer. She had an idea.

If she couldn't have a real pet, maybe at least she could make one.

Chapter 2

It took her weeks to finish her project. Sewing the different components together was the trickiest part. Online knitting tutorials made it look easy, but her pieces never turned out as neat and symmetrical as she wanted them. The dog came out lopsided, some of its legs longer than others, its head tilted as if to listen. It was also smaller than she'd planned, small enough to fit in the palm of her hand. It had floppy ears, a low-slung body and a thin tail. Its black button eyes shone. Its stitched muzzle tipped up at the corners in a smile.

"Hi there." She cupped it in both hands and held it at eye level. "Now all you need is a name. What should I call you?"

She looked around for inspiration. She was sitting at her crafting table, which stood in front of her window for better light. The wind was shaking down a rainfall of yellow leaves from the oaks and poplars on the college campus across the street. Her table had an autumnal look too, scattered with scraps of colour: yarn balls in a basket with knitting needles stuck into them, spools of rainbow thread, a pincushion shaped like a hedgehog, her ivory sewing machine…and on a coaster out of the way stood a mug still half full of warm cocoa. The drink was practically the same colour as the little dog in her hands.

"I'll call you Cozy," she decided, and kissed it on the nose. "Pleased to meet you, Cozy."

It looked back at her out of blank button eyes. Even in the pride of her accomplishment, she felt a surge of longing that made her catch her breath.

"I wish you were real," she whispered.

In that moment, something happened that she could never explain afterward.

A strong wind swept through the room, fluttering stray threads and blowing Norah's hair back from her forehead. It was not cold as she would have expected in autumn, but warm, and did not smell of the falling leaves outside, but of fresh rain and lightning, like a spring thunderstorm about to break. The lamp flickered. Something like a static shock crackled from Cozy's fur into her hands.

She gasped and dropped the dog onto the table.

It somersaulted, scrambled back up onto its four feet, and barked.

She was dreaming. She had to be dreaming. She'd fallen asleep face down at her crafting table and would wake up tomorrow morning with a crick in her neck and a still-unfinished knitting project, because none of this was possible. She squeezed her eyes shut and rubbed them with her knuckles.

Cozy was still barking.

Yipping, really. Its voice was as tiny as its body. It scampered over to her, tail wagging, and put both front paws on her elbow, which she had propped on the table. It sniffed her sleeve. She was wearing a lavender sweater she had knit herself. Her woolly dog was sniffing her woolly sweater. It was too bizarre.

She burst out laughing.

"You're impossible," she said, offering her fingertips to the dog to sniff instead. "You know that, right?"

Cozy jumped up to lick her hand with a woolly pink tongue. It tickled. She hadn't even used any pink yarn.

"Oh, that reminds me," she said. "I can't keep thinking of you as *it*, can I? Not as long as…"

The words *you're alive* still sounded too bizarre to be true; focusing on little details felt safer. She rummaged in her sewing kit for spools of ribbon and set them in a row, all the colours she had left: pink, green, purple, blue, silver, and gold.

"Are you a boy dog or a girl dog, Cozy?" she asked, unconsciously falling into the sing-song tone she'd heard mothers and pet owners use. "Or a different dog altogether? Go on, don't be shy. You'll look cute in any of them, I promise."

Cozy pounced on the trailing end of the blue ribbon, unspooling it as it went. Norah grabbed the spool, snipped off the other end with her scissors, and with some difficulty—"Hey, c'mon, hold still!" she coaxed as the creature wagged his whole body along with his tail—she got a loose bow tied around his neck.

"There you go, boy," she said, rather breathlessly adjusting the bow. "You look very handsome."

Cozy lifted his head high and pranced around the table as if he quite agreed.

The Summons

A Salt and
Light Anthology

Chapter 3

Norah was not a morning person.

Her alarm was set for 7:45, a quarter hour before her shift started at work. She'd drag her bleary-eyed self out of bed, stumble to her computer, log in, type an obligatory *Good morning* to her colleagues, and take her shower and breakfast while keeping her ears open for the chime of message alerts. This early in the day, there generally weren't any. She suspected she wasn't the only one who needed a few hours to wake up.

On that morning, however, it wasn't the alarm that woke her. It was tiny paws scampering over her pillow and a nose nuzzling her face.

She yelped and sat bolt upright, grabbing the pillow to throw.

Whatever it was whimpered.

It wasn't a mouse, as her half-asleep brain had assumed. It was Cozy, backing up with his tail between his legs and looking up at her with wide, glistening eyes.

"Sorry," she gasped, lowering the pillow. "Didn't mean to scare you."

Cozy's tail and ears lifted. He cocked his head to the side and whined inquiringly.

The Hand-Knit Dog

"I'm okay." She took a few deep breaths to calm her racing heart. "So…I guess it wasn't a dream, eh?"

Besides Cozy himself, the evidence was all over the room. She'd put her yarn basket on her nightstand as a miniature dog bed for him, but just like a real dog (as far as she knew from watching online videos), Cozy must have preferred to sleep on her bed. Her pillow had a dent on the upper left side, smaller than anything her own head could have made. He'd also knocked several yarn balls down and sent them rolling around the floor, leaving a tangle of trailing threads. In the grey light of early morning, falling in stripes through the window blinds, it looked like a rainbow had lost its way trying to get back to the sky. It would take ages to untangle.

Norah was torn between pullingher own hair out with annoyance, and sitting speechless with awe all over again that Cozy was alive at all.

How in the world had it happened? Did she have some kind of powers without realizing it? If so, why wouldn't she have realized it earlier? Maybe it was the yarn she'd used to knit him. She'd always felt that there was something special about the Second Chance Shop, although until now, she had assumed it was simply due to the eclectic merchandise and the kindness of the staff. There had to be a logical explanation.

Cozy jumped from the bed to the nightstand, then up onto the alarm clock, whose bright orange digital display read 6:41 AM.

He danced on the buttons. Static crackled, followed by a pop song, then a traffic report.

"Yeah, no, you're right," Norah mumbled, shaking her tousled hair out of her face and her confused thoughts out of her head. "I really should get moving."

Cozy didn't leave her much time to theorize about where he came from. He tried to follow her into the bathroom ("NO!"), started a tug-of-war with one of her socks while she was getting dressed ("That's not a squirrel, buddy, give it back"), and got himself smeared all over with hazelnut spread during breakfast ("Did you have to leave fuzz all over my toast?"). Norah dunked him in the kitchen sink to wash him. He yelped and squirmed and came out looking like a drowned rat, ears and tail drooping, smelling of wet wool and lavender dish soap. He didn't stop shivering until she rubbed him down with a towel. It was astonishing to actually feel him snuggle into her hands. She couldn't remember raising her voice so much—or laughing so much—in the whole of the past week.

She sat down at her computer flushed and smiling, with a fresh cup of tea on the coaster beside her. She felt wide awake and professional as she logged in, poised to wish her teammates a good morning at eight a.m. on the dot.

Naturally, Cozy chose that moment to knock over her tea.

A brown lake flooded her keyboard. Drops spattered the

screen and ran down in rivulets. By the time she managed to react, it was already dripping down to the floor. She lunged for a box of tissues and started cleaning, imagining the tea soaking into the circuits and possibly ruining her laptop forever.

Cozy perched on the shade of her desk lamp, his tongue hanging out in what she considered a shameless grin.

"You're kind of a disaster, aren't you?"

Cozy yipped.

"Please don't do that again. This is my job we're talking about."

Cozy jumped down onto the newly wiped desk and started chasing his tail in circles, which struck Norah as an uncomfortably accurate metaphor about her job.

She sighed in relief when she saw that her computer was still working. Her teammates had posted a stream of good morning GIFs on the group chat: steaming coffee cups, blinking kittens, cartoon characters peering out from blankets. She never knew how to react to these, but at least this morning she had something to say.

Norah Eckart 8:08 AM

Sorry I'm late. My dog knocked over my tea cup and it spilled all over.

Joaquim Ribeiro 8:09 AM

my dog did that once too :D

Florence Choi 8:09 AM

ooh tell me about it
I swear my little monster cat tries to claw up every device I have
lol

René Tremblay 8:10 AM

didn't know you had a dog @Norah, what kind? Mine's a goldendoodle named Chewie

Norah blinked at her screen. She couldn't remember the last time she'd had such a personal conversation with her colleagues; it must have been before the pandemic, if at all. It warmed her more than the spilled tea could have done.

Norah Eckart 8:12 AM

His name is Cozy. He's hand-knit.

Heart emojis popped up immediately under the text, as did a few question marks. Self-consciously, she added:

Norah Eckart 8:13 AM

I just say that because he's fluffy.

I don't know what breed he is.

She reached over to run one fingertip along Cozy's fluffy back. He flopped over and showed her his belly to scratch instead.

"But now I really have to get to work," she told him, smiling from ear to ear.

One of the things Norah had always looked forward to (or dreaded, depending on the weather) about having a dog was taking said dog out for walks. Cozy might not have the traditional excuse for going outside—as far as she knew, he didn't eat or leave droppings—but there was no reason why they shouldn't do it anyway.

Although seeing this tiny creature scampering around the floor, tied to an improvised leash made of tailor's elastic, she did have a few misgivings.

"You'll be careful, right? You won't get stuck in a bush or fall in a hole or…or let a cat get you?"

Yip, yip!

"Also…if we run into other people, try not to let them get a close look. You can pass for a normal dog…a really small sheepdog puppy, maybe? But only at a distance. The last thing I want is to draw the wrong kind of attention."

Cozy, whose ears had gone flat and his tail limp as she spoke, shook himself all over and lifted them up again. He bounded over to her and tugged on her pant leg with surprising strength.

"Whoa, okay! Guess that means we're going."

Before opening the door, however, she paused to check her reflection in the hallway mirror. It had come with the apartment—full-length mirrors were not something she considered necessary—but today, with Cozy's leash wrapped around her wrist, she felt unusually conscious of how people might see them.

She saw a pale, plump woman wearing pale blue drawstring pants and a pale pink sweater with lumps in it (one of her early projects). The eyes behind her glasses were an undecided shade between blue and grey. Her brown hair was growing shaggily out of its bob. No, she definitely wouldn't draw attention. She had been resigned to that since high school. Cozy, on the other hand…

She smiled as she watched him leap up toward the doorknob, his ears and the ends of his blue bow flapping from the jump. Even in the dim light, his wool was the colour of fresh hot chocolate. She might not have been beautiful, but at least she could make beautiful things. She still had no idea where Cozy's inner beauty could have come from, but his outer beauty was definitely hers.

She felt for her keys in her pockets, locked the door behind her, and stepped outside.

Cozy ran ahead of her down the corridor, pulling the leash taut, then circling back again. The corridor was empty. So was the elevator; so was the lobby. On a Saturday morning, she imagined, everyone else behind these rows of closed doors was either still asleep or having breakfast. She pictured older couples smiling together over the newspaper comics; young parents frying chocolate chip pancakes for their children's Saturday brunch; student roommates nursing their hangovers with warm towels and steaming pots of coffee. All imagined, of course. She couldn't really know.

The wind ruffled her hair as she and Cozy stepped outside. It smelled of evergreens. It swept through the maple trees, shaking loose a rain of golden leaves that twirled and fluttered before landing on the sidewalk. Cozy stopped to watch, his head tilted up as high as it would go, his black eyes open wide. A leaf almost his own size landed on his head. He sneezed. Norah grinned.

"Morning, Norah." She spun around.

Jean perched on a ladder overhead, pruning the spruce hedge in front of the building. Clipped twigs were already scattered over the grass; he must have been at work since sunrise. His flannel shirt, a dark green tartan that blended into the hedge, clung to his back. He waved his shears at her.

"Hi, Jean."

"Beautiful day, eh?" He swept the shears out in a wide half circle. "Look at these leaves! My wife, she always says it's like living in a Van Gogh painting."

"Oh, yeah. It's beautiful." She held up the hand holding Cozy's leash. "I'm taking my dog out for a walk."

Jean's smile faltered as he looked down at her feet.

Norah ducked her head, remembering how just a few weeks ago he'd told her no furry pets were allowed in the building. "I promise he won't give you—or the other tenants—any trouble. He's a good dog, aren't you, Cozy? Just…a little bit unusual."

Jean frowned. "Hmm. I can see that."

Norah noticed that the tugging on the leash, which she'd felt ever since she'd picked it up, was suddenly gone. She couldn't remember when it had stopped. She looked down to find Cozy standing next to her left shoe, not moving, doing his best impression of a lifeless toy.

She twitched the leash. He fell over sideways. She scooped him up from the pavement and held him close.

"What the—" she caught herself muttering under her breath. "Cozy, what's going on?"

She jumped at the metallic creak of the ladder and the thud of Jean's boots on the ground. He walked up to her, pushing back his cap to meet her eyes. His own eyes, a dark hazel she had never noticed before, looked back at her with something far too much like pity. She tucked the still motionless Cozy into the crook of her arm and began backing away.

"Norah, are you okay?" His French accent, usually worn down from years of living in an English-speaking neighbourhood, seemed to deepen. "It's just, I never see you with anyone else in this house, I know you spend a lot of time alone, and I know it's not my business, but maybe…maybe you need to talk to someone?"

He must have thought she was delusional. Her face burned.

The sane thing to do, she knew, was to stand her ground and give the man a reasonable answer, preferably with dry eyes and a calm voice. She could say she'd only been joking and didn't actually believe a hand-knit plushie was alive. She could tell him the name of the video channel where she'd found the instructions and the kind of needles she'd used, point out where one of Cozy's ears was higher than the other, and bore Jean senseless until he understood that she did in fact know the difference between an animal and a craft project. She could even tell him everything she knew about the night of Cozy's creation, which—though unlikely to convince him—was at least closest to the truth.

All her reasonable answers, however, rushed up into her throat at once, where they congealed into an aching knot until she couldn't say a word.

She turned and ran.

Behind her, she dimly registered Jean calling her name, but she didn't turn around. Her red-hot haze of humiliation swallowed everything else: the crunch of leaves underfoot, the smell of earth and evergreen sap, Cozy's inert figure clutched in one hand, everything but the sidewalk in front of her. She ran until her legs burned, her lungs heaved, and a stitch stabbed her in the side. Then she stumbled into a plodding walk, head down, lurching aside just in time when cyclists rang their bells, parents pushed their babies in strollers, or dog walkers (normal dog walkers, she assumed) came by. Their golden retrievers, shepherds, and Pomeranians didn't even sniff in Cozy's direction. How was he still not moving? What was wrong with him?

She dragged herself past the college campus, up the road that led to the neighbourhood cemetery, and into one of the narrow little bike paths that wound behind houses and between streets. It was quiet there, which meant fewer people to see her crying. Tall birches shielded her from the gravestones on one side, and a high wooden fence from the backyards with their swing sets and swimming pools on the other. The ground was uneven, shaped by birch roots into a lopsided staircase and covered in a carpet of browning leaves. She scrubbed her tear-stained face with her free hand so she could see where she was going. With every step, her mind became a little clearer. Unfortunately, so did the knowledge of what a fool she'd made of herself, running and crying like a toddler. She was thirty, for pity's sake. Every time she thought she'd outgrown this, it happened all over again, and why? Because she'd tried to connect with someone, and inevitably failed.

"Oh, Cozy," she whispered, leaning back limply against the fence. "What's wrong with me?"

Cozy bit her.

It was like a shock of static electricity, right where he'd wriggled around and closed his jaw over the skin between her thumb and pointer finger. It stung. She yelped.

Then, static electricity or no, she cuddled him to her cheek.

"You're alive!" she sobbed. "I thought you were…I don't know what I thought."

He licked her tears away with his ticklish woolly tongue.

"Please tell me you didn't do that on purpose. You made Jean think I'm hallucinating you. When I said not to draw attention, I didn't mean play dead. I know that's a thing dogs do, but don't you normally have to train for it?"

Cozy flopped theatrically sideways in the palm of her hand, only to bounce back upright and wag his tail.

"You're impossible." She tapped him on the nose. "I'm starting to think I didn't really create you after all."

He tilted his head inquiringly.

"If I had, I'd've made you speak human."

He let out a high-pitched howl, which she could have sworn meant he was as frustrated with her as vice versa. Before she could even begin to figure out why, though, he jumped down from her hand and trotted along the path, negotiating the tree roots as nimbly as if he'd known them for years.

"You're right," Norah said ruefully. "Let's go home. But, uh, Cozy?"

Yip?

"Can we circle around and go through the back door? I just can't look Jean in the face again."

The little dog let out a surprisingly heavy sigh.

The Hand-Knit Dog

221

The Golden Years Residence might not have been golden (it was red brick, actually), but it did remind Norah of a castle. It was only three floors high, but its gabled windows, roof peaks, and rounded corners suggested towers and turrets. Precisely clipped flowerbeds and a neat row of recycling bins all spoke of forethought and maintenance. Norah, squatting down to retie her shoelaces in the driveway, felt ridiculously young in all the wrong ways. As she squinted at the roof peaks pointing up into a cluster of rain clouds, she was tempted to turn right back. She had signed up to volunteer here weeks ago, before Cozy, when she'd thought spending time with an elder might be nice. She had even managed to pass an interview with the program coordinator via video call, and exchange emails to set up this appointment. That was before the incident with Jean had reminded her just how bad she was at face-to-face interaction.

Cozy stuck his head out from inside her purse and growled.

"I know," she whispered, her breath hot inside her face mask. "Too late to cancel now. Not when she's already waiting."

She pictured a lonely old woman in a room that smelled like sanitizer, waiting by the window for a visit that never came, and hauled herself upright with a growl as determined as Cozy's.

"Just…please stay in the bag, okay? Remember what happened

the last time someone saw you."

She cringed all over again at the memory of her meltdown. Cozy growled like a tiny motorcycle, but huddled down into his faux leather hiding place anyway. She would have rather left him at home but, fuzzy ball of chaos that he was, she doubted the apartment would still be in one piece if she left him alone. Besides, she needed some moral support.

"Sorry about this." She patted the purse. "I know you don't like it. We can play fetch by the river as long as you want later. I promise."

Cozy yipped sharply. She tucked the purse under her arm and walked into the building.

"Hi," she said, spraying her hands with the dispenser next to the front desk. "I'm Norah Eckart. I, um…I have an appointment?"

"Eckart…how do you spell that?"

Norah spelled it. The receptionist, a slim woman younger than her whose mask matched her white uniform polo and whose hair was tied back in a perfect bun, clicked and scrolled through her computer and looked back up with a nod. "You're here for the visitor program?"

"Yes."

"Great!" The receptionist's mask barely muffled her professional cheer. "If you wouldn't mind filling this out, just in case?"

She slipped a questionnaire form through a small gap in the plastic barrier. Norah fished a pen out of her purse (trying to keep a straight face when Cozy licked her fingers) and ticked *No* for all the boxes: whether she had a criminal record, whether her vaccines were up to date, whether she'd experienced any symptoms in the last fourteen days or been in contact with anyone who had.

"Thank you!" The receptionist nodded as she took back the form. "Now, just sign your name in the guest book and sign out again when you leave, and that's it!"

The guest book sat on a podium next to the desk, with a vase of chrysanthemums beside it. It was bound in what looked like brown leather. Norah wished she had a fountain pen to sign it with instead of her sputtering ballpoint, but the receptionist didn't seem to care.

"You can go right on through. They're waiting for you in the lounge."

"Am I late?"

"Not at all, you're right on time. Enjoy your visit!"

Norah wondered if she should thank the receptionist, decided the pause had gone on too long, nodded stiffly, and shuffled through the doors to which the other woman had pointed.

The lounge was a wide, warmly lit room with red walls, mint-green armchairs grouped around little tables, and an electric fireplace. A snack table was set up along one wall, with pots of tea and coffee and trays of pastries, conscientiously labeled as to nut, gluten, and sugar content. Pumpkins, maple leaves, and even plastic skeletons (which Norah considered rather tactless, before reminding herself not to judge) decorated the room. Walking past a black cat plush toy on the mantelpiece, she put a quieting hand on her purse, but to her relief, Cozy didn't seem to be the kind of dog who barked at cats.

"Norah, yes? Good to see you!" Bonnie, the program coordinator, came bustling toward her with an eye-crinkling masked smile. She was in her fifties, with long, fluffy grey-blonde hair and a Halloween-orange dress. "Getting chilly out there, eh? Did you drive?"

"I walked."

"Oof!" Bonnie grimaced. "If you need a ride home, just call me." She made a gesture as if to take Norah's arm, remembered the six-foot rule, and backed away. "Anyway, the snacks are free, so help yourself, and then I'll introduce you to Lisette. She's so looking forward to meeting you."

Norah trailed after Bonnie as she weaved between armchairs and tables, the coordinator chatting with everyone they passed, white-haired elders and the people who must be their visitors, ranging from Norah's age to high schoolers. As Norah dodged purses, canes, walkers, wheelchairs, and oxygen tanks, clutching a coffee cup in one hand and a cranberry muffin in the other, she wondered uneasily if Bonnie's assertion was true. With an age gap this wide, what would they even talk about?

They stopped in front of a chair in the far corner, partly turned away from the others. The first Norah saw of her assigned conversation partner was her shock of candy-apple-red curls, so much brighter and thicker than the dark eyebrows underneath that they had to be a wig. The skin of her face was thin as tissue paper. She put aside the cup she was holding and peered up at her visitor through a thick pair of cat-eye reading glasses. These and her mask made her expression difficult to read, but she did not look especially welcoming.

"Lisette, honey," Bonnie scooped up the cup and frowned at the black liquid, "you know what the doctor said about coffee."

"Still Madame Martineau to you." The older woman's voice was deep, raspy, and French. "And the coffee hasn't killed me yet."

"This is Norah, your visitor." Bonnie's hands hovered on either side of Norah's shoulders. "She's a knitter like you, so you should have plenty to chat about! I'll just leave you to get to know each other, okay? See you later!"

The coordinator bustled off, her orange skirt swirling around her, leaving Norah face to face with a stranger.

"Parlez-vous français?"

"Un peu."

What Madame Martineau said next was so fast that Norah's rusty schoolgirl French gave out, and all she could do was shake her head helplessly.

"English then," said the old lady, with a long-suffering sigh. "Sit down. You're so tall, you make my neck hurt."

Norah dropped into the diagonal armchair, deposited her cup and muffin on the little table between them, and gathered her purse (and Cozy) into her lap.

"So, um, you like knitting too?" she asked, clinging to Bonnie's suggestion for an icebreaker topic.

"No. I hate it," said Madame Martineau, with a snort. "But all the things I like to do, my body and the doctors don't let me. I can't dance, can't run, can't eat my favourite food…but one must do something to pass the time in this place."

Norah shrank into her chair.

"And you, what do you do to pass the time?"

In order to not mention knitting again, Norah said, "I'm a video game language tester."

The old lady cackled.

"No, really. That's my job. I'm like a…like a book editor, just for video game texts. I make sure everything is spelled correctly and, like, doesn't take up too much space…"

Norah trailed off. The hours she spent struggling through a blizzard of error messages when a game refused to download, or watching her avatar die a dozen bloody deaths in pursuit of a single screenshot, sounded so surreal even to her that she couldn't blame Madame Martineau for not believing it.

Cups clinked. Spoons rattled. The coffee percolator bubbled. People laughed and talked. A grandfather clock let out five sonorous chimes. Five p.m. Half an hour to go and they were already out of things to say.

She cradled the purse in her lap. *Cozy, what do I do?*

The purse wriggled.

Before she could stop him, say something, or react in any way, her hand-knit dog took a flying leap onto the table, and another one into Madame Martineau's lap.

Her mask crumpled inward in a gasp…then blew out with delighted laughter.

"Un petit chien!" she crowed. *"Comme c'est mignon…mais…"* She lifted the tail-wagging Cozy up to eye level, squinted at his button eyes and wool threads, and shook her head. *"Incroyable."*

Norah's French might have been rusty, but she understood that much. She stared at Madame Martineau staring at Cozy. It would be hard to say who was more astonished, except the dog, whose tail was a positive blur of joy at being petted and admired. Norah, torn between awe and worry, kept an eye out for anyone who might laugh at them for playing with plushies at their age, but no one seemed to have noticed the impossible thing happening in the room.

"You can…see him?" Norah whispered, leaning on the edge of her seat. "You can see him moving?"

"I'm not blind yet, young lady. And even if I was, I can feel him. *N'est-ce pas, mon brave?*"

"Do you know…do you know how this happens? He's been with me for weeks and I still don't understand—"

"Nobody understands a miracle," said Madame Martineau, opening her cupped hands to let Cozy run an obstacle course around the table. "That is not the point of them. Just be grateful. And don't shut him up in your little bag."

Cozy bobbed and weaved between cup, muffin, and a stack of sudoku magazines like an athlete, making the most of being outside. Madame Martineau glared at Norah through her cat-eye glasses in a way that made the younger woman feel smaller than the dog.

"I know…but the last person I showed him to thought I was losing my mind."

"You care too much about what other people think." Madame Martineau's mask puffed out in a sigh. *"Eh bien,* I did too when I was your age. That was before I learned what a waste of time it is."

She slumped back in her chair, as if too much awe at once had tired her, and fumbled for Norah's coffee cup on the table, a white cup with a yellow Golden Years logo like the one Bonnie had taken away earlier. Cozy, still galloping around the table, jumped in front of the cup and guarded it like a soccer goalie, hackles raised, button eyes narrowed to determined slits. Madame Martineau drew her hand back.

"Hey! What are you, my doctor?"

"He gets like that," said Norah, with a shrug. "Protective, I mean. At least he didn't spill it. I had no idea before he showed up that miracles would take up so much laundry."

The two women caught each other's eyes over the tops of their masks and laughed together. Cozy relaxed his guard and jumped back into Madame Martineau's lap.

"You're not so bad," the old lady said abruptly, scratching the dog between the ears. "You can come back next week…what did you say your name was?"

"It's Norah, Madame. And he's…well, I call him Cozy."

"Funny." Madame Martineau's laugh rustled like dry leaves. "Nice to meet you, Norah and Cozy. Call me Lisette."

Chapter 6

"Tabarouette!" Lisette grumbled as her knitting slipped down her needles.

She was making a scarf, or so she said, but "scarf" was a generous word for the cherry-red tangle of knots in front of her. Norah had been coming to visit for weeks now and hadn't seen it grow much longer, let alone tidier. She had been too timid to say anything, but she couldn't watch this waste of perfectly good yarn go on without at least trying to salvage it.

"You need to hold it like this." Norah held out her hands. "Can I show you?"

Lisette handed over the needles with an impatient snort, but her eyes were alert as she watched Norah demonstrate. They were sitting together on the navy blue sofa of Lisette's suite at the Golden Years Residence, which was an odd mix of institutional and homey. Norah could see at a glance what had belonged to Lisette and what was original to the suite. The latter was in all neutral colours—the navy blue couch, brown wooden furniture, ivory carpets, oatmeal-coloured walls—while the former was as colourful as Lisette's wig, which today was platinum blonde. Purple, turquoise, and magenta cushions with gold embroidery decorated the couch, one tucked behind Lisette's back, one placed horizontally for Cozy to curl up on. A red poinsettia bloomed in front of the window sill, ignoring the rain that streaked the glass and the wind howling outside.

"Ah, I don't know how people do this." Lisette's technique had been improving, but now she tossed the knitting aside. "Why do *you* do this?"

Norah couldn't tell whether that was a rhetorical question or a real one, but ventured to answer anyway, "I guess…because it makes sense to me. The patterns, the repetition… I know you think it's boring, but I like it," with a shrug. "Also, I just love the way yarn feels."

"Who doesn't, eh?" Lisette ruffled Cozy's ears.

"My mom taught me when I was little." Norah remembered the smell of her mother's rose soap, warm steady hands guiding hers as she held the needles, and a patient voice telling her it was okay to make mistakes. "When I call her on FaceTime, we always show each other what we're working on, and Dad's like, *I just live here*." His bemused, but proud expression as he scooted his chair back to make room for his wife's half-finished throw blanket still made Norah smile.

"Hmph. Your mother's a lucky woman. My son, he never wanted to learn anything from me." Lisette's smile crumpled into a frown.

"You have a son?" Norah asked. Cozy lifted his head and perked up his ears.

"Had."

"Oh, I—I'm so sorry," Norah stuttered.

"Tch, he's not dead. We just don't talk to each other."

Lisette picked up a framed photograph, which had been lying face down on the side table, and looked at it for a long moment. Norah had noticed the hidden picture before, but never asked; she'd assumed the old lady's unsteady hands must have knocked it over by accident.

It was an early colour photo, still bright, even though it had faded with age. It showed a young Lisette with auburn hair and a flowery dress, her hands on the shoulders of a little dark-eyed boy. He looked up at the camera without smiling, an old-fashioned brown leather satchel held in his arms. It may have been Norah's imagination, but he already looked like a traveler getting ready to leave.

"What happened? If you don't mind my asking?"

"Lots of things. It was complicated…but it all went—how do you say?—pear-shaped, when he married an Anglo girl. It was the nineties referendum, you see? We were so close to getting our independence, and then what does he do? He brings the enemy home for dinner. That's how it felt to me."

For once, Norah's poor communication skills worked in her favour. Half a dozen answers crowded into her head—none of them respectful, all of them in English—but they all stuck in her throat. Her face must have said it all, though—or else it was Cozy, whose button eyes were fixed on the old lady with deep disappointment—because this time, it was Lisette's turn to duck her head and look awkward.

"Oh, I know, I know…I let stupid politics get in the way instead of just letting him be happy. I understand that now, but it's too late. I mean…there's the internet now. If he wanted to, he would have found me."

Cozy, who had been listening intently, trotted across the sofa to where Lisette held the photo in her lap and delivered one of his static shocks to her bare wrist.

"*Aïe!* What was that for?"

Norah rubbed her own wrist ruefully as she remembered. "When he does that to me, it's usually because I'm feeling sorry for myself. He doesn't like that."

Lisette's glare could have stripped paint.

"I mean, not that that's what you're doing," Norah backtracked. "It's just… What if your son feels the same way? What if he thinks *you* don't want to find *him*?"

"Enough!" Lisette's mask filled out with the force of her raised voice. "You don't know what you're talking about."

"I'm sorry." Norah jumped up from the sofa and began to

back away, bumping into a chair and reaching back to keep it upright. "I didn't mean…"

"You think you can tell me how to live my life, when you can't even live yours? Get out! Both of you, get out!"

Norah ran for the door.

Looking over her shoulder to make sure Cozy was following, she saw the little dog still trying to get through to Lisette. She had torn off her mask and hunched in on herself in the corner of the sofa, breathing heavily, swatting Cozy away when he tried to nudge the photograph with his nose. Was it Norah's imagination, or did she look pale?

"Cozy!" Norah hissed, struggling into her rubber boots and raincoat at the same time. "Come on!"

Cozy's paws dragged across the carpet, but he went.

"Um, Lisette? Can I still come back next week, or—"

"OUT!"

Lisette's anger blew them both out the door, down the hall, and into the storm, which felt considerably safer. Norah tucked Cozy into her coat pocket and made her damp and shivery way home, wondering how many times she could fail at communicating with other human beings before she gave up, and also hoping against hope for Lisette to be okay.

Chapter 7

From: knitpicker@videotron.com

To: lmartineau@videotron.com

Subject: (no subject)

Dear Mme Martineau,

[DELETE]

Dear Lisette,

[DELETE]

I was just wondering if our appointment is still

[DELETE]

I'm sorry about all the things I said. You're right, your family history is none of my business, but I was just trying to help

[DELETE]

It sounds to me like you and your son are both as stubborn and unreasonable as

[DELETE]

You had no right to push Cozy away like that

[DELETE]

I know Cozy and I upset you, but was that all or was it something else? Are you sick? Do the Golden Years staff know? Are you taking care of yourself?

[DELETE]

I miss you.

[DELETE]

From: knitpicker@videotron.com

To: bonnie.oreilly@goldenyears.com Subject: Appointment

Hi Bonnie,

Could you please check with Mme Martineau to confirm today's appointment? Is it still at 5:30?

Norah

From: bonnie.oreilly@goldenyears.com

To: knitpicker@videotron.com

Subject: Re: Appointment

Dear Norah,

I'm sorry to tell you that Mme Martineau passed away last night.

She will be much missed among the residents and staff. On behalf of us all, thank you for bringing so much joy to her life in the short time you knew her.

I will contact you later with details regarding the memorial service, as soon as it can be arranged.

Yours sincerely,

Bonnie O'Reilly

Activity Manager

Golden Years Residence

The Summons

A Salt and Light Anthology

238

Norah stared at the blazing white screen of her laptop until her eyes stung.

The last person she had known who died was her maternal grandmother. They had never been close, either emotionally or geographically, so for Norah it had been more of a second-hand grief on her mother's behalf. Still, even second-hand grief could hurt. She remembered her mother's emails, written by the bedside of a woman too medicated to even recognize her family, every spelling mistake hinting at blurred eyes and shaking hands. She remembered the phone call that gave the news, Norah and her mother both crying, her mother apologizing for her tears even at a time like this.

Usually, her parents were the first (and only) people she could call when she felt like this, but how could she tell them about Lisette without telling them about Cozy? One look at their faces on her screen and the whole story would come tumbling out. They wouldn't believe her. Her father was a skeptic when it came to anything supernatural. He liked to read horoscopes aloud just to laugh at how inaccurate they were. And her mother would worry. No, she couldn't tell them.

Her eyes, nose, and throat burned with tears. Knowing she was crying for selfish reasons—not for Lisette Martineau, without whose bright colours the world was a drabber place, or for her unknown son, who might never find out that his mother had regretted their estrangement—made her cry even harder.

She felt a distant tickle on her hand. It was Cozy. From the corner of her eye, she saw him jump from her desk to her bookshelf, where she kept a stack of knitting magazines. He started pulling them down, some landing on the floor, some on her desk. Their pages fluttered open like leaves in a storm, showing her brightly coloured photographs of every pattern she had ever wanted to learn.

She found this neither comforting nor funny. The body she had knit for him felt hopelessly too small for a sorrow this size. More than that, looking at him made her angry, and it did not take her long to realize why.

"You knew Lisette was sick." Cozy whirled to look up at her.

"That's why you didn't want her to drink coffee, because she said her doctors wouldn't let her. That's why you didn't want to leave her last Friday. Why didn't you make it clearer? Why didn't you…I don't know, warn us? Is it because you didn't want to, or…because you couldn't?"

Cozy lifted his head and growled low in his throat, turning his back to her to face something she couldn't see. Was he growing taller, or was she imagining it? Her imagination had been overworked for so long where he was concerned…and so had Lisette's.

"I knew she was sick. I had a feeling, I just didn't pay attention. I could've talked to Bonnie or the nurses—that's what Bonnie told me to do in the interview, remember?—but I didn't.

It was never really you, was it? You never noticed anything Lisette and I didn't notice first. She was so old, and I'm so…" Norah's self-disgust couldn't even find the words for what she was. "We must have…somehow…made you up together."

Cozy static-shocked her ankle. She felt nothing. In a world where death could slowly destroy everything you loved, a hand-knit dog couldn't possibly be alive.

"You're not real," she whispered, and to herself: "He was never real."

A movement of her foot sent Cozy falling sideways.

Norah fell to her knees on the floor, realizing what she had done. She hadn't reasoned away her grief after all, only left herself alone with it. Real or not, her best friend was gone, and it was all her fault.

"I'm sorry," she cried. "I didn't mean it! Please, come back!"

But the toy never moved.

The Hand-Knit Dog

241

The Second Chance Shop was a nonprofit that sold people's donations to raise money for medical research. It had once been one of Norah's favourite places in the city, because you never knew what you might find: vintage patterns from the 1950s, hardcover editions of forgotten children's books, a sturdy food mixer when your old one broke. Now, though, she felt like a grave robber as she walked in, surrounded by the relics of past lives. Those gold-rimmed plates painted with forget-me-nots had been someone's "good china", saved for special occasions. That quilted jacket in the window display had wrapped around someone and kept them warm. Would anyone ever buy them, or would they just sit there until they were tossed into a landfill?

Stop that, she ordered herself. *In and out, that's all. You don't have to stay here.*

She dumped an old duffel bag, stuffed with all the half- finished yarn balls, needles, and magazines it could hold (as well as one hand-knit dog), into the bin by the door and turned away. It felt like leaving an arm or leg behind, but at least if she couldn't create, that meant no more unhealthy fantasies about her creations.

A sudden movement at the corner of her eye made her jump.

It was the trunk of a car being pushed open in the street

outside, which she could see through the shop window. The car was a little green Beetle, no longer new, but not pristine enough to qualify as vintage. She had seen that car before, parked in the garage of her own apartment building. It belonged to Jean—and there he was, approaching the shop with his arms full of cardboard boxes, and his wife Linda walking beside him with even more boxes and bags.

Norah ducked behind a shelf.

She hadn't spoken to Jean since that time she had tried to introduce him to Cozy, and the caretaker had pitied her and she had run away in tears. It was all the more humiliating now to realize he had a point. She probably did spend too much time alone if she had to resort to knitting an imaginary friend.

She missed Cozy so much, her breath caught in her chest.

She heard rustling noises as Jean and Linda placed their boxes in the bin with care. Peering through the gaps between the stacks of kitchenware on the shelf, she watched them. Jean looked smaller and older without his newsboy cap. With the hood of his jacket pushed back, she could see how far his hairline had receded. Linda's grey bob had been tousled in all directions by the icy wind. Their heads were bowed over the bins.

Both of them wore face masks, a sight that pierced Norah's heart. Jean had often complained about the masks, and had stopped wearing them in public as soon as city regulations allowed it. If the couple wore them now, it meant that something must have happened to frighten them, to remind them how vulnerable they were. Norah's own mask trapped her hot breath against her face, half smothering her with the smell of detergent. She never left home without it.

If Cozy were real, she caught herself thinking, he would do something ridiculous any second. He would static-shock her, pull her forward by his leash, start barking for the entire store to hear. Anything rather than let her hide behind this shelf from people who had been kind to her.

She was never sure afterward how it happened, but somehow she was straightening up, walking towards Jean and Linda, and lifting her gloved hand in a characteristically awkward wave.

"Hi," she mumbled through her mask.

"Oh, hello," Linda said warmly as her husband nodded a greeting. "You live in our building, don't you? Haven't seen you in a while. How are you doing?"

Norah had no idea how to answer that. Saying she was fine would be an obvious lie, but she could hardly inflict the whole dreary story on someone who might have only asked out of politeness. Instead, she said the first thing that popped into her head, which was the same thing she had wanted to say to Jean for weeks.

"I'm sorry I was so rude the other day. I know you were just trying to help."

"Eh? Oh, that. Don't worry about it." Jean patted her gently on the arm with his gloved hand. "It's been a hard few years for all of us."

That was a weight off Norah's mind. Mask and all, she could breathe easier than she had in weeks. "Can I, um…can I help you with those?" She pointed to the open trunk of the Beetle outside, which still had baggage piled inside.

"Thank you, dear," said Linda over her shoulder, gesturing for Norah to follow. "That would be very nice."

Norah hurried out of the shop after her, hefted the biggest bag she saw, and carried it back to the bin regardless of the handles cutting into her fingers. Jean and Linda did the same with a cardboard box they carried between them, slamming down the trunk with one free hand each.

"So…are you fall-cleaning?" asked Norah, once the last box had landed in the donation bin, in an attempt to make conversation. "I know spring-cleaning is a thing, so…"

"Hmm, you could say that." Linda shook back her hair and stretched her arms as if they ached. "Fall-cleaning. Interesting word."

"My mother…" Jean cleared his throat and looked down at the boxes. "We've been sorting through her belongings. It's…"

"It's been a very emotional time, as you can imagine," said

Linda, squeezing her husband's arm. "We weren't on speaking terms for so long, and then for her to reach out to us so suddenly just before she passed away… Well, it was a shock."

Norah was reminded so powerfully of Lisette, she had to cling to the edge of the bin for balance.

"What if your son feels the same way?" she had asked the older woman. *"What if he thinks you don't want to find him?"*

"Enough! You don't know what you're talking about!"

Was it possible? Could Jean's mother and Lisette have been the same person? Could Linda be the "Anglo girl" the old lady had disapproved of? Could she really have changed her mind after such a complete rejection?

"That reminds me…" Jean reached into his coat pocket and held something out. "She asked me to give you this the next time I saw you. I could have left it in your mailbox, but…it felt too important for that."

It was a bright red scarf, hand-knit, loose in some places and knotted up in others, barely long enough to wrap all the way around. Norah could almost hear every frustrated curse, feel every cramp of aged and inexperienced fingers, every fiercely determined stitch that had gone into it from beginning to end.

"Lisette Martineau?" she breathed, holding it in both hands.

"That's right."

"She made this…for me?"

Jean's smile was invisible under his mask, but his voice was warm. "She said… How did she say it? A young lady and a little dog finally talked some sense into her. She talked about you so much that I recognized you at once."

"She wanted to thank you," said Linda. "And so do we."

"Really?" Norah's hands shook as she draped the scarf around her jacket collar. She let out a breathless little laugh so as not to cry. "I'm just so glad she found you…and, and so sorry you lost her…you know what I mean?"

"We know," Jean and Linda said at the same time.

Norah stood in front of them with her hands in her empty pockets, wishing she had something—anything—to give them in return. If only she hadn't dumped her knitting supplies, at least she could make them something. If Cozy were real…

She felt soft yarn under her fingers, where only seconds ago, there had been nothing but the polyester slickness of her pocket.

Floppy ears. Button eyes. A nose. A satin ribbon collar with a bow at the back. Four legs. A fluffy tail.

She had packed him into the bag. She had tied the handles in a knot right over him. She had tossed him into the bin along with everything else…hadn't she?

Now here he was in her pocket. She did have something to

give, after all.

She withdrew the hand-knit dog from her pocket and held him out to Jean and Linda.

"For you," she said.

"Oh no. Thank you, but no." Jean's eyes softened even as his hands went up; no doubt he recognized the dog from their last encounter. "You don't have to…"

"I want to. He's… Lisette liked him. It was something we had in common. I would've given it to her if…if she was still here, so…I'd like you to have him. Please."

It was Linda who took Cozy from her, petted him, and held him up to her cheek.

"The grandkids will love this," she murmured. "Amazing work, dear. Did you really make this on your own?"

"Sort of," said Norah. "I guess I was… inspired." "Well, thank you. We'll take good care of him, I promise."

They said their polite goodbyes, and as they turned away with Cozy tucked under Linda's arm, the last thing Norah saw of him was his tail.

It could have been her imagination, but she could have sworn it wagged.

The Hand-Knit Dog

249

Afterword

By Maria Fedina

As we are told to think on what is good and true and beautiful, and as we live in an age of cynicism and irony, in a world that too often scoffs at truth and goodness and sincerity, it seemed fitting that Keepers of the Gate's first anthology should be a collection of fairy tales.

Though fairy tales are generally associated with children, no one who's actually read the Brothers Grimm or Hans Christian Andersen, let alone Lewis or Tolkien or George MacDonald, can honestly say that fairy tales are just for children. Of course, the morals behind children's stories tend to be fairly simplistic—be kind, be good, don't talk to strangers—and it's natural that as children grow, they are eager to put away childish things and move on to more mature reading material. C. S. Lewis acknowledged this desire to appear grown up in his essay, "On Three Ways of Writing for Children," and in his dedication to The Lion, the Witch, and the Wardrobe, as he supposed that his then fourteen-year-old goddaughter was "already too old for fairy tales." Even so, with age comes wisdom, including the wisdom to not let self-consciousness get in the way of enjoying a good story, to appreciate truth wherever it may be found, and to recognize that there are few genres better suited to conveying deep and profound truths than the humble fairy tale.

In our collection, Addy was a sweet and simple vignette of

pure friendship and kindness, while The Girl Who Chased the Sun and The Boy in the Castle were a mix of awe and terror, love and sacrifice. City of the Sun painted a picture of hope in times of darkness; The Hand-Knit Dog, wonder in the face of dull and dismal reality; The Masque of the Ald-King, the value of contentment, wisdom, and discernment, and of course, a caution against being too trusting of strangers. Though the stories are fantastical, the virtues they highlight are real and well worth remembering for readers of all ages.

Thank you for reading, and we hope you'll join us on our next adventure.

www.ingramcon
Lightning Source
Chambersburg PA
CBHW080653010
48977CB00000